"Still the most beautiful woman in Montana," said a hauntingly familiar voice.

"Oh!" Lily wasn't sure whether she gasped or shrieked. Two men rose from their chairs to face her. One made her knees weak and turned her mind to a thoughtless puddle of emotion.

"Lillabeth," Randall said. "This man claims to be your husband."

Lily didn't hear him, couldn't see him. She saw only Saige.

He was thinner, but his eyes had not lost their humor, nor his lips their boyish grin. Best, or worst, his laughing voice had not lost the power to make her tingle right down to her toes.

"Hey, Blue," Saige said. "This man claims to be your fiancé."

Dear Reader,

Harlequin Romance would like to welcome you back to the ranch again with our yearlong miniseries HITCHED! We've rounded up twelve of our most popular authors, and the result is a whole year of romance Western style: cool cowboys, rugged ranchers and, of course, the women who tame them.

This month marks the welcome return of Catherine Leigh to Harlequin Romance, with her wonderful new romance, *Something Old, Something New*. Catherine hails from the great state of Montana, where wild cowboys and ranchers are part of the scenery.

Catherine loves to hear from her readers. You can write to her at:

P.O. Box 774
Ennis
MT 59729

Look out in October for Barbara McMahon's *Wyoming Wedding*.

Happy reading, partners!

The Editors
Harlequin Romance

How the West was wooed!

Something Old, Something New
Catherine Leigh

Harlequin Books

TORONTO • NEW YORK • LONDON
AMSTERDAM • PARIS • SYDNEY • HAMBURG
STOCKHOLM • ATHENS • TOKYO • MILAN
MADRID • WARSAW • BUDAPEST • AUCKLAND

For all the chapters she's critiqued, for all the spleen she's let me vent, for all the brainstorming sessions she has shared, most of all for filling an empty space in my life with laughter, joy of living and love, this book is gratefully dedicated to:

Barbara Johnson Smith

ISBN 0-373-15672-3

SOMETHING OLD, SOMETHING NEW

First North American Publication 1996.

Copyright © 1995 by Catherine Lee Donich.

PROLOGUE

LILLABETH Alexander peered through her camera lens at the Fourth of July parade in Deep Water, Montana, and a shriek rose in her throat. The man standing across the street, behind the streamers and flags of the Little League float, bore such an eerie resemblance to her husband, Saige Alexander, Lily couldn't speak.

Saige was dead, wasn't he? If not, where had he been the past seven years? And why had he never once communicated with her—not since that last loving letter from Caracas, the pages long since disintegrated by her tears?

Lily stared. It wasn't Saige. This man didn't have those golden streaks she'd always loved in Saige's hair. And his face was too thin. In fact, his whole body was too thin. Except...those gray eyes...

No, it couldn't be.

After all, life had gone on. Not right away, of course. It had taken an agonizingly long time for Lily to begin painfully putting her life back together. But she had. And now... Her mind whirled.

"Are you all right, darling?"

The words came from Randall Carver III, her fiancé. She and Randall planned to wed next month, the day after she could have Saige declared legally dead, freeing her to marry again.

Randall took her elbow. "You look like you've seen a ghost."

CHAPTER ONE

RANDALL pressed his lips to Lily's brow as if checking her temperature. "Lillabeth, have you been out in the sun too long?"

"S—Saige," Lily murmured dazedly.

Randall's brows lifted. "I beg your pardon?"

Lily raised her camera again, this time aiming the viewfinder directly at...whoever that was across the street. "Randall, I think that's...Saige over there. Behind the float."

"Don't be ridiculous, Lillabeth. Saige is dead." He made a self-deprecating noise. "I should have known better than to discuss all that with you yesterday. But I had no idea it would upset you this much."

"You didn't upset me, Randall," Lily said without looking up.

"Of course it did, my dear. You don't need to understand all the procedures for having your husband declared dead." Randall gave her arm a squeeze, jiggling her camera. "I should have just told you where to sign and handled it myself."

Lily patted his hand on her arm, thinking how many things Randall had "handled" for her the past few years. At first, in the aimlessness of her depression and grief, she'd let him take charge of her life. But she was stronger now, and his "assistance" had begun to make her feel helpless. She'd tried to explain that to him yesterday.

"I wanted to know, Randall."

"The only question you asked was what would happen if he came back after we were married." Randall spoke as he would to a distraught child. "He's not coming back, Lillabeth."

Lily's thoughts tumbled frantically, but she kept her finger firmly pressed to the auto-advance, silently cursing the fact that the parade was in her way and that the film in her camera was Tri-X 400, which turned out such grainy black and white prints—perfect for newspaper photos, but rotten for the purpose of identifying a man at a distance.

But then, she wasn't here to go sleuthing. She'd only come to cover the parade for the Deep Water *Register*. After getting roped in to help Randall's mother, Kokie, with her annual Independence Day barbecue, Lily wanted to skip the parade this year.

But Lily's boss at the paper, Pernell Quillan, whom everyone called Pen, had refused to let her out of the task. No one else, he'd insisted, could take decent pictures *and* develop them *and* write the story before tomorrow's deadline. It was times like this, Lily was sorry Pen had succeeded in turning the paper from a sleepy little weekly into a real daily.

Times like this? Lily thought.

When had there ever been another time like this? Never before, and never again, Lily hoped, would she look across the street and see a dead man. A dead man she had once loved, loved to distraction, loved without question every day of her life—well, at least since the second day of kindergarten.

"Lillabeth?" Randall shook her arm, dislodging her finger from the shutter button. "Where is this apparition?"

Lily lowered the camera. Her heart pounded oddly and she felt cold, or was it hot? She started to point at the spot where he had stood. The man had disappeared, and the crowd filled his place on the curb so quickly, Lily wondered if she'd really seen him at all.

"He's gone," she said, her voice echoing with emptiness.

"Of course he is, my dear." Randall slipped his arm around her shoulders.

Lily leaned against him, gratefully. Her knees felt like they wanted to quit holding her up.

Taking another roll of film from her bag, she decided she'd better pay some attention to the parade. She stared unseeingly at the Side Saddle Club, now passing in front of her. She'd always loved these women, clad in their nineteenth-century riding habits.

Saige hadn't.

He'd seen the club, the way it gloried in the past, as just another way to tie him to Deep Water. When his father recovered fully from gall bladder surgery, Saige hadn't wanted anything else to trap him on the ranch, a life that had dissatisfied him since childhood. He'd taught Lily to ride sidesaddle himself, but he asked her not to join the club.

After he'd left for South America, Lily, too, had wished to avoid anything that might increase her attachment to Deep Water, which she would soon have to leave. Saige had interviews lined up at five multinational corporations and would surely get a job at one of them. As soon as he did, he'd send for Lily. He'd written almost daily, the pages filled with his excitement and craving for adventure.

Then the letters stopped.

And Lily wished her life would stop, too.

In the years since, Lily had slowly learned to numb the pain. Anger had taken its place, then that, too, had numbed. But the anguish of not knowing... Dear heaven, how many million times had she prayed for the answer?

Only... did she want it *now*? Now that she'd learned to accept the loss, to bear the hurt, to find a new life, a stable life, a *secure* life—did she want to find Saige *now*?

"Lillabeth," Randall scolded. "You're exposing that whole roll of film. Shouldn't you put it in the camera?"

"Yes, I just..." Lily looked at the roll of film still in her hand. "Randall, I've seen so many of these parades, I could write the story in my sleep. I think I'll just run up to the newspaper and develop the first roll." She prayed she'd taken enough shots before the stranger appeared to fill a page of the paper.

He brushed his lips against her cheek. "I'll be at my office. I've got to pick up those contracts for Mother to sign at her barbecue."

Lily nodded vaguely. "Right, I'll meet you at your contract."

Randall took her upper arms and peered at her beneath the brim of her visor. "Lillabeth, I'm not sure you're all right. We mustn't let this sort of foolishness distract you. Perhaps I'd better come with you."

"No, no," she assured him. "I'm fine." She put a hand on his smooth-shaven cheek, feeling all his stolidity that had first drawn her to him. "I'm just a little rushed. See you, sweetheart."

A little rushed and a little out of my mind, she thought. *But I won't think about it till I get these pictures printed.*

In the dim light of the darkroom, Lily watched the face appear beneath developing solution, sure it could not be her husband's. The man wasn't simply thinner than Saige had ever been—his face also bore an expression of age or pain that she simply couldn't associate with the passionate, carefree man she'd loved. And his eyes...

A tremor shook her as she stared harder at the eyes, feeling her own fill with tears. If this was Saige, he had suffered hardships past her imaginings. Oh, if only she had a decent picture!

But it couldn't be Saige. When she pulled her gaze back to take in the whole, not simply the eyes, disbelief eased her mind. This was simply a man with a superficial resemblance to Saige, who happened to have eyes rather like his, who had appeared at a time when—as Randall had pointed out—she was thinking quite a bit about him. She trailed a finger across the damp print, down the outline of the face, wondering if there had ever been a time, if there ever would be a time, when she wouldn't think about Saige Alexander.

No! everything inside her screamed, as she controlled her tears with anger. That time was now. She hadn't thought about Saige for months...well, days. Not until she'd seen this stranger. She thought about Randall now. Stable, kind, protective Randall.

Thoughts of Saige hurt. She didn't want them. Even before he left, loving him had been intense, but never comfortable. His discontent with the ordinariness of their life, with the daily demands of ranching, had kept her constantly on edge— always afraid his adventurous streak would overcome his sense of familial duty and he'd insist they take off again for parts unknown.

And then his disappearance! Lily shook off those memories fast, before the too-familiar agony could pierce her heart and shatter her new-found peace.

Randall was right. She didn't need to think about having Saige declared dead. Randall could handle it. She'd simply sign wherever he told her and return Saige Alexander to the back of her mind with the other fading memories from her childhood. All widows had to do that sooner or later, didn't they?

Lily dropped her parade story and pictures on Pen's desk, firmly closing her mind's eye to those other photos. But a wayward thought whispered to her that she was glad that man wasn't Saige, glad time and untold adversity hadn't ravaged her wonderful, laughing husband into a stranger she hardly recognized.

When she pushed open the door to Randall's outer office, rustling from his inner office told her someone was with him.

"Put that picture down, damn it," she heard Randall bark. "It's nothing to do with you."

Lily knew what picture he meant—the one he kept of her on the corner of his desk. Randall loved the picture. It had been taken last year at the end of the summer banquet at the golf course, the night Randall and Lily had announced their engagement. Just as the photographer snapped the picture, Randall had taken her shoulders and turned her to him to tell everyone how glad he was she'd finally agreed to become his wife.

In fact, as only Lily knew, she'd been staring up at Randall in surprise that he would make such an announcement a year before their nuptials could take place. She'd thought he understood that she loved Saige's memory too much ever to divorce him, no matter how long he'd been gone. But champagne, something she rarely drank, had blurred her astonishment into adoration in Randall's eyes.

"Still the most beautiful woman in Montana," said a hauntingly familiar voice.

"Oh!" Lily wasn't sure whether she gasped or shrieked.

She ran to the door of Randall's office. Two men rose from their chairs to face her. One made her knees weak and turned her mind to a thoughtless puddle of emotion.

"Lillabeth," Randall said, his voice tight with disapproval, "this man claims to be your husband."

Lily didn't hear him, couldn't see him. She saw only Saige.

He *was* thinner, his face pale and lined. The golden streaks had disappeared from his light brown hair, replaced by a patch of gray just above his right ear. But his eyes, his wonderful gray-green eyes, had not lost their humor, nor his lips their boyish grin. Best, or worst, his laughing voice had not lost the power to make her tingle right down to her toes.

"Hey, Blue," Saige said. "This man claims to be your fiancé."

Lily stretched a hand toward him. "Sa—" She couldn't quite complete the word before black spots took over her vision and her knees quit altogether.

She opened her eyes to find herself lying on Randall's chesterfield couch, staring up at the only two men she'd ever loved, who hovered close above her. Suffocatingly close. Putting a hand on Saige's chest, she pushed him back and sat up. Before she could remove her hand, Saige covered it and held it tight against him. The beating she felt beneath her palm flowed into her and matched the beat of her own heart.

Saige was definitely alive! But as she gazed into his once beloved, too thin face, the emotion that swept through her with stunning force was anger. Rage. Fury! How dare he do this to her!

Deliberately Lily removed her hand from his. Her gaze never left his eyes as she pulled back her arm and slapped his cheek with all the strength she could muster. Saige saw it coming and closed his eyes. He winced at the pain, but he didn't flinch or shield himself from the blow. The red imprint on his face brought tears to Lily's eyes.

"Damn you!" she cried, pounding her fists on her knees. "How dare you? How dare you abandon me . . . *us*, then simply . . . show up? Do you know what I've—what your parents— Do you have any idea . . ." She covered her face, biting her lip to hold back tears. "We thought you were dead!"

"I know." Saige pulled her hands down. He hadn't rubbed his cheek, which must be throbbing, but he took her hand and massaged the sting from her palm. "Believe me, I know. Seven years of hell. For me, too."

"You, too?" Lily jerked her hand free. "At least *you* knew you were alive." She swallowed the lump in her throat, which didn't move an iota. "Where the *hell* have you been?"

Saige flicked his gaze at Randall, then back to her. "Not here, Blue. Not now."

"Not now?" she exclaimed. "When? In another seven years?" She took a deep breath. "Have you been in Caracas all this time?"

Saige's lips thinned as he shook his head.

"Did you stay in Venezuela?"

"No," he said. "I left, but not—"

"Left Venezuela?" she cried. "Without telling me?"

A torrent of undiluted pain and fear and desperation swept through her as she remembered the horror of trying in vain to search a foreign country from thousands of miles away. Now it seemed she'd searched the *wrong* foreign country.

"When you disappeared—" her voice quavered but she kept it under tight control "—I thought I would die, truly die, from grief and terror. Your mother helped me, I helped her. But in the end, we had to bury you and all our memories." Her control slipped as her voice grew shrill. "Now I find you just took off on some ... jaunt!"

Saige's eyes darkened with pain. "It was no jaunt, Lily. I—"

"Don't say another word, Saige. There's nothing you can say to make it all right. Nothing. Nothing!" She glanced at Randall, his lips white from tension. "Do your parents know?"

Guilt tightened Saige's haggard features as he shook his head. "I expected them to be at the ranch. I didn't know where they'd gone till I talked to your ... lawyer here."

"I'm more than her lawyer," Randall sputtered. "I'm her fiancé." He tried to move closer to Lily on the couch but Saige sat between them. "Call me what you will, Alexander, but it won't change anything, no matter what you think." He sounded angry and ... vulnerable.

"Oh, Randall." Lily wanted to take his hand, but she would have to reach across Saige's body. She didn't think she could bear to touch him and heighten her awareness of how thin and hard he'd grown.

She stood and walked to the window, gazing out at the little town that had always been home for her. Despite Randall's denial, Saige's return must change things—how could it not? But what?

Was she still engaged? Married? What did she feel? She couldn't tell. A flash flood of emotions was overwhelming her ability to think.

Saige came toward her. Lily knew it was Saige. Something indefinable about the sound of his movements, the warmth of his breath on the top of her head. She didn't question her ability to know these things. She certainly couldn't be faulted for recognizing Saige's hands on her waist. He was her husband, damn it, of course she knew his touch.

"I understand," Saige said softly.

"You don't have a clue!" Lily said with more bitterness than she'd known she possessed.

"When you're ready to talk," Saige said, "I'll be at the ranch." He pressed her waist, gently, persistently, till she faced him. "There's one thing you're going to hear whether you're ready or not. I never stopped loving you, Blue. Not for a single second. You never left my thoughts. I'd have done *anything*, increased my own pain a thousandfold, if I could have lessened yours."

"Don't," Lily whispered, anguish tearing at her chest. "Please don't. It's too late. You hurt me too much . . . too many times."

"Let her alone and get out," Randall snapped from across the room. "You've upset her enough."

Saige released her and started toward the door. He stopped, his back ramrod stiff. "No."

In two strides he was in front of her again, his arms sliding around her waist. He pulled her to him. "Some things have waited long enough."

"Oh, no, you don't," Randall growled, rising from the couch.

"Oh, yes, I do," Saige whispered to Lily.

One kiss, she thought, instinctively stretching up to meet him, *one kiss cannot wipe away seven years of pain and rage and confusion and terror.*

But her body didn't believe her. She had ached for this touch too long, too desperately, to deny herself now. Whimpers of joy and longing burst from her as she wrapped her arms around Saige's neck and opened her mouth to his. Want, frantic all-consuming want, engulfed her.

She knew every inch of him. He'd changed, hardened, grown far too lean. Yet his broad hands traveling up and down her spine molded her to a body she'd have recognized in her sleep. His lips and tongue played that old teasing game with hers that no one else played, because no one knew the rules but Saige.

Lily had dreamed this kiss, a thousand times, a thousand thousand times. She'd imagined it everywhere—in their bedroom, on Main Street, at the airport, on the summit of Sphinx Mountain. But though her dreams had been fueled by real memories of Saige and his kisses, the flesh-and-blood reality of his touch took her with the power of a tidal wave. She couldn't fight him; she didn't want to.

Randall began to shout. Lily had no idea what he was saying, but the sharp sound was just enough irritant to keep her from letting Saige drag her to the couch—or the floor, for that matter—and make love to her there and then.

Saige must have felt her dawning awareness of Randall. As he lifted his head, Lily struggled to return to the moment. Something had changed in the gray-green irises that smiled at her now. Relief, that was the difference. And a measure of confidence. It softened the creases of suffering in his face, the haze of fear in his eyes.

And it made her mad.

But she couldn't speak. What could she say after her wanton reaction? Unhand me, you cad? Your place or mine, lover? Neither seemed right.

The corner of Saige's lips twitched up as if he could read her thoughts. "God, I've missed you, Blue. I never thought I'd feel you this close again."

Lily closed her eyes and summoned all her strength. "You won't another time," she said, stepping out of his arms.

Randall was beside her to pull her to him. "That's the last time you'll put your hands on my future wife," he said in a peremptory tone Lily had never heard him use before. She wondered if he meant it for her or for Saige.

In Randall's stable embrace, Lily's frantic pulse began to ease. The inner peace she'd gradually acquired during her engagement to Randall had been vanquished by Saige's return, but she prayed not forever.

She wrapped her fingers tightly around Randall's arm, longing for some of his sturdy calm. "Randall's right, Saige," she said, her voice trembling ridiculously. "I...you're... It's too late."

A flare of anguish dimmed the hope in Saige's eyes, making Lily ache with guilt. He reached out a hand and cupped her chin, rubbing his thumb roughly across her lips. "When you're ready."

With an effort, she jerked her head away. "I won't ever be ready."

Saige's jaw tightened. "You kiss like you still love me, Blue."

"No, Saige. Not anymore. Not after what you did to me." At last, her tears began to flow in earnest. "Just go!"

Saige left her, sobbing into Randall's chest and clinging to him for support.

CHAPTER TWO

"How could you allow him to kiss you that way, Lillabeth? Right in front of me. Do you know how that made me feel?"

Randall turned off the highway onto the gravel road that led to his mother's summer cabin. Though Lily knew Kokie's winter home in California was far grander, she still could not bring herself to call a five-bedroom house with a detached guest house a cabin even if it was built of logs.

"I'm sure it hurt your feelings, Randall," Lily said, patting his knee. "I'm sorry for that. But you can't worry that it will ever happen again. I mean, I don't have any other dead husbands hidden to return suddenly from the grave and kiss me."

"Kiss you insensible, Lillabeth."

Lily sighed and pulled down the sun visor to examine her destroyed eye makeup in the mirror. She'd washed her face and removed traces of running mascara, but her eyes were still red. She folded up the mirror. At least her face looked better than Randall's shirt, but he'd promised to borrow one from his father's closet when they got to Kokie's barbecue.

The barbecue! The last place on earth Lily wanted to go right now was Kokie's party—*any* party. How could she act politely sociable when she felt as if an emotional railroad had just flattened her on the tracks? She longed for solitude and quiet to try to come to grips with Saige's return.

"Lillabeth!" Randall's voice demanded her attention. "Did you hear what I said?"

"He was my husband, Randall. He kissed me before. And...more than kissed me. You have to accept that." She cocked her head at him. "I thought you had."

"Is."

"Is?"

"Not *was* your husband." Randall downshifted, turning onto his mother's private road. "*Is* your husband."

As they crawled forward at a few miles an hour, Lily thought for the hundredth time that having a Lamborghini in a town with only two paved streets was foolish. On the other hand, came the errant thought, at least Randall was here, in Deep Water, and planning to stay. Any craving for adventure he might have, he could satisfy by speeding along the highway in a fast car.

"Is," she murmured in agreement.

Suddenly Lily understood why Randall had insisted so vehemently that they attend this party.

It wasn't just—as he'd asserted—that his father only visited Deep Water a few times every summer and they ought to see him. Unlike Lily, who wanted to go home and hide, Randall wanted to be as public as possible tonight. He needed to declare to the world, at least his own world, that, no matter how married Lily still was legally, she had not changed her mind about intending to marry him next month.

"Oh, Randall, I'm married! What do I do now?"

Randall spared her a glance and his tone softened. "Just what I should have insisted you do last summer. You'll have to divorce him."

A jolt of acid twisted her stomach. Her mind filled with thoughts of Warren and Grace Alexander, Saige's parents. Lily loved Warren almost as much as she did her own father, Dana Harmony. Dana had worried—with good reason—about Saige's peripatetic nature, but he loved him like a son.

And Grace. Lily's eyes began to tear again. She didn't remember her own mother, who had died when she was a baby. But she and Grace had been fast friends since the day they met when Lily was eight. Later, when her body started changing, then through the years she'd dated and had been married to Saige, Lily had thanked God again and again for giving her a friend and mother-in-law like Grace.

Oh, they were all so tied together by pasts in common and loves so intense and tangled! When Lily told Grace and Warren she meant to have Saige declared dead and remarry, they decided not to come home from Arizona at all this summer. How much worse would they feel, would Dana feel, when she told them she was *divorcing* Saige? Divorcing the man she'd loved since kindergarten, the man whose disappearance had nearly killed her, divorcing him just as he came back to her.

How could she do it?

"Lillabeth." Stiff as he sounded, Randall's tone carried an underlying note of hurt that Lily could tell he was trying to hide. "Don't you love me at all? Was I really only a substitute for... the real thing?"

"Oh, Randall, no." When she'd first heard Saige's voice in Randall's office, Lily had thought her heart would break. Now it felt ripped in two. "I love you just for yourself. What I feel for you... It's completely different and unique."

"I am different from him, Lillabeth." Randall pulled the car onto a wide spot in the road. "I'm not like him at all. If that's what you want again, you shouldn't marry me." He turned off the ignition and stared out the windshield at the mountains in the distance. "But you have always led me to believe, my sweet, that you never wanted that sort of relationship again."

"I don't," Lily said emphatically. She undid her seat belt and squirmed as close to Randall as she could get. "I couldn't do that again. But can't you understand how I feel?"

"No, truthfully, I can't at all." Randall sounded as rational as he always did. "I know nothing about the man except that he craved excitement and hurt you terribly. As you know, you have never bothered to tell me his good points, *why* you loved him so much."

"I didn't think you wanted to hear those things."

"Quite right." He gave her a small smile. "I don't want to hear them now, either." Suddenly he wrapped her in a fierce hug, holding her tightly to him over the console between them. "Lillabeth, I love you so much. Tell me again you love me, too."

"Of course I do, Randall."

He rubbed her back. "You don't really believe he'll stay in Deep Water this time, do you?"

Lily felt as if he'd just doused her with a bucket of ice water. Her mind had barely begun to grasp the reality of Saige's return. Now Randall had voiced the ultimate question about Saige before she'd even thought of it.

Saige had come to Deep Water to find Lily and his parents. But he hadn't said anything about wanting to stay. Even if he did, could she believe him? Would anyone? What about next year, when

Deep Water had paled again into his boring ordinary old hometown?

"No," she said dully. "He won't stay."

"People don't change, Lillabeth."

"No." She freed herself from Randall's entwining arms. "I just...don't know how to get divorced."

"Of course you don't, sweetheart." He gave a comforting little chuckle. "I'm a lawyer, remember. I can handle all that."

At Randall's words, Lily felt that old numbing urge to sink into the glove leather upholstery and let him, once again, "handle" something difficult for her. But this time she couldn't.

"I don't mean the legalities, Randall. That part seems easy enough—" she gave him a grateful look "—with you helping. I mean...Grace and Warren and my dad. They'll never forgive me. Or understand it. And telling...Saige. Filing papers on him, when he's already so... Well, he looked awful, didn't you see? And Randall, what about Kokie?"

"Mother?" He arched his brows.

"Yes. You remember how she reacted last summer when you announced our engagement and she thought you were going to marry a divorced woman." She wondered if Randall knew how unwelcome Kokie had made her feel. "She didn't exactly...approve."

Randall cupped Lily's face in both his hands. "Sweetheart, she hardly knew you then. You two have gotten quite close this year, and she's really terribly fond of you. She's told me many times she approves my choice." He pressed his lips on hers. "You know how much I want you. I adore you, Lillabeth. The only question is, do you still want to marry me?"

Lily looked into the warm brown eyes that had grown so familiar to her. Nothing had changed, had it? Saige wasn't dead, but he had abandoned her and hurt her, badly. She could never again feel the way she used to, never again be so young and foolish, never again trust him with her whole heart. Randall's love was milder, perhaps, but easier to live with for the long term. She could count on him always to be there.

"I still want to marry you."

A broad smile warmed his well-bred features. "Then it's decided." He turned to the steering wheel. "I'll start divorce proceedings next week."

The sun stabbed knife-edged rays of light through Lily's window, making her turn her face into the pillow with a groan. The movement brought her more pain and a serious roiling in her stomach. Clamping her teeth and lips together didn't help. Besides, flexing the muscles in her jaw made her temples pound.

Lily didn't want to face the light of day. Why, oh, why hadn't she had the sense last night to close the shades? She should have closed the window, too. The shrill chirp of magpies sounded like the Liberty Bell inside her head.

Champagne. Ugh. What had possessed her? She should have known better—she *did* know better. Who had champagne at a picnic, anyway? Only Kokie. Sitting in tubs of ice, as though it was beer. Which was certainly the way Lily had treated it. Randall had warned her after the second glass when he'd brought her that plate of pinky shrimp mold and—

Lily's stomach lurched, and so did she. Off her bed and down the hall to the bathroom. She hadn't thought she could run so fast with her head throbbing.

When at last she slumped to the hall floor and leaned against the wall, she realized her phone was ringing. How many times had it rung? No matter. She obviously wasn't going to get to the receiver before her answering machine did.

She heard Randall's voice, speaking in that self-conscious tone he used on these machines. "Lillabeth, sweet, I was worried about you. You looked like death warmed over when I dropped you off last night. I hope your blond little head is still attached to your curvy little body." He chuckled at his witticism, though it made Lily want to swear. "Don't worry about Mother. She understands and isn't a bit upset with you. Call me when you've recovered. I'll let you sleep until I hear from you."

Lily tried to grasp the import of this message. A few things were clear. Randall found her raging hangover amusing, just as he had the only other time she'd drunk alcohol in his presence. That did not endear him to her this morning. And Kokie was upset about something. What?

The act of concentrating made her wish she'd stayed in bed. Her stomach had settled some, but her head hurt worse. Hazy memories of the barbecue floated back. She remembered clearly Kokie's look of horror—dignified horror, but horror nonetheless—at hearing that Lily was still married to a living, breathing man.

In fact, it was that look that had prompted Lily to accept the first glass of wine. She'd known it was a mistake. She'd anticipated this morning at the first sip. But anything had seemed better than listening to Kokie try to explain her dismay that someone Lily loved was alive.

Lily leaned her head into her hands as the phone began to ring again. She didn't consider trying to reach it. But when she heard the voice of her boss on the tape, she pushed herself off the floor and wobbled to the instrument on the wall of the kitchen.

"Pen," she groaned, snatching up the receiver as she clicked off the answering machine. "It's Lily." She glanced at the clock above the sink. "Was there something wrong with the story? Weren't there enough pictures? I—"

"The story's fine, Lil," Pen assured her. "Already on the streets, in fact. I just wanted to let you know I heard about your husband."

"You heard what?" she asked, suddenly anxious. With Deep Water's rumor mill so active, Pen might know more about Saige's missing seven years than Lily. The thought made her distinctively uncomfortable.

"Just that he's back." Pen paused. "I don't suppose you'd like to interview him about where he's been for the *Register*?"

"No!" Lily said adamantly. "No, no, *no*!"

"I didn't think so," he said. "But . . . well, you understand, someone will. I thought I'd better warn you. Not today. I'll give you a chance to take this all in first. But tomorrow if I can catch him, or the next day at the latest. I have to. He's news."

Lily sat down hard on the oak stool Saige had made in high school shop class, one of the few things she'd brought to her apartment from their house at the ranch. "Yes, Pen. I see." She wondered if newspapers always invaded privacy so shockingly. It had never seemed this excruciating on the other side of the interview. "Thanks for letting me know. Do me a favor, will you?"

"If I can."

"Go yourself. Please." She rubbed at her throbbing temples. "I know everyone in the valley will be frantic with curiosity, but . . . I'd hate to have the story sound like the *Enquirer*."

"Request granted, Lil. I meant to do that anyway." Pen's coffee cup clicked against the phone. "By the way, you've got some vacation days coming. Now might be a good time to take them. If you get my drift." He hung up without making her come up with an answer.

Lily folded her arms on the kitchen counter and leaned her head onto them. She couldn't, she absolutely could not learn where her own husband had been for seven years by reading about it in a newspaper. Pen's warning and his offer of time off to hide after the story came out were kindnesses she appreciated deeply.

But kindness or not, Pen's call meant she had to see Saige today. She groaned again. Today!

Still, she might as well. Even last night she had realized that sooner or later, when Randall was not hovering beside her, she would have to hear the whole story of where Saige had spent the missing years. And why. Replacing another groan with a grunt of determination, Lily pushed herself to her feet and headed for the shower.

The ranch looked much as it had since Lily was a little girl. Watching seasons change on the land was one of the things she loved about living in Deep Water. The year she and Saige had spent in New York, she'd watched the seasons change by what was flushing down the gutters: brown rain, dirty slush—did snow *ever* stay white in New York?—touristy litter.

Summer to Lily meant these fields beside the road, where impulse sprinklers shot huge semi-circles of water over waving alfalfa. When she drove into the yard, fear shot through her. The ranch house looked completely deserted, unlived-in, unwelcoming. Not even the shutters had been removed.

Dear heaven, she hadn't dreamed Saige, had she? He really had come home last night...hadn't he? She'd felt him, his strong arms, his soft lips, his beating heart. She had, she knew she had.

Panic seized her. It couldn't have happened again, could it? Had Lily turned Saige away with her hurt? He wouldn't simply disappear again, would he? No, God, please, no. Don't let him disappear again!

CHAPTER THREE

LILY jumped out of her car and ran toward the back door. Saige opened it before she crossed the porch. The sight of him filling the doorway of the house they'd shared as husband and wife, still warm and breathing, still here, still real, not dreamed, overwhelmed her rational thinking.

"Saige!" She threw herself into his arms and buried her face in his neck.

He brought his arms hard around her waist. "Lord, Blue, I'm glad to see you."

"I was afraid," she whispered into his throat, not wanting to look at him or face her feelings. "I thought...the house looked so dark...the shutters...I was terrified you'd gone again, and I'd never know." She straightened as if to pull out of his arms, but he held her to him.

"Never." She felt his heartbeat quicken. He stroked a hand down her back beneath her blond ponytail, still damp from her shower. "I'm never leaving again, no matter what you do. I mean it." His hand pressed warmth against her spine. "Do you believe me?"

She shook her head. "No."

"No? I'll prove it to you, woman." He tangled his fingers into her hair.

The pressure, gentle as it was, against her scalp sent stabs of pain pounding to her temples. "Ooh!" she gasped.

Saige let go immediately. Taking her face between his palms, he tipped her head back and met her gaze. The smile that curved his lips was sympathetic. And knowing.

"Look at those eyes," he said. "They used to be blue, didn't they? I've remembered them blue for seven years. Don't tell me all this time they were red?"

"I thought seeing a ghost at the parade a good enough reason to indulge in, um, a glass or two..."

"Looks like a whole bottle to me." He stroked with infinite softness across her eyelids. "Champagne?"

"Uh-huh."

Saige's smile faded as he uttered some guttural oath. "I'm sorry, love. Seven years of pain and the first thing I do when I get back is hurt you again."

"I did this to myself, Saige."

"My fault, though." Opening the door, he gestured her inside.

The darkened house felt wonderful to her aching eyes. But everywhere she looked, something reminded her of the life she'd shared here with Saige—the life she'd left behind when she moved into her apartment in town.

"I should have called you," Saige said. "I tried to do it the way it'd be easiest for you. Really. I thought you'd take it better in person than from some disembodied voice over the phone." He made a noise of disgust. "I should have known better."

He urged her into the only chair not covered by a dust sheet. "You never could drink." Carefully he removed the hair band from her ponytail, letting her hair fall loosely over her shoulders.

"Don't," she whispered. "I can't let you do this."

"It's medicinal, love."

Saige rubbed hard in the shallow indentations above her eyes. She winced as he increased the pressure, trying to turn away—just as she always had. He gripped the back of her head, holding her facing him—just as he always had. When he released her, the throbbing had stopped.

For the first time that day, Lily opened her eyes wide with relief. "No one else can do that."

"No one else knows you so well."

Lily wanted to look away from the awareness in Saige's eyes. Suddenly she was angry with herself for putting them in this position again. She had made her decision.

"Please," she said, trying to sound distant, "don't do or say anything else to remind me how well you know me."

Saige rolled his gray-green eyes and said nothing.

"Just tell me." She drew her hair band from his hands and began twisting it through her fingers, watching it slide over one knuckle, under another. "Tell me how you could ... leave ..." She stopped, unable to keep her voice from trembling.

Saige's shoulders stiffened as an expression of guilt crossed his face. He stood, holding out a hand to her. "I'd better make coffee," he said. "We could both use some."

Lily started to shake her head then thought of the comfort of the ranch kitchen. She remembered how many conversations she'd had there—with Grace as well as Saige—that had brought her pleasure. Hearing Saige's story while she sat in this chair and he knelt before her might ignite emotions she wasn't prepared to handle.

Saige didn't wait for her answer. Ignoring his proffered hand, Lily rose and followed him into the kitchen. She sat on another of the oak stools at the counter, watching him putter with coffee and filters and water.

"I'll probably make it too strong for you," he said. "I got used to stronger stuff in ..."

Lily's throat muscles seemed frozen. "In?" she managed to croak.

Saige stood at the sink, filling the pot. Water began to run over the rim and down the sides. He shut off the faucet. "In," he agreed, his back still to her. "Not in Caracas."

Lily's mouth opened soundlessly then closed again. She felt like a fish. "You left Venezuela."

"I did." Saige started the coffee brewing and faced her. Leaning across the counter, he took her hands. "But you knew I wasn't there anymore, right? You must have looked for me." He paused. "Venezuela and the United States have diplomatic relations. Surely they helped you."

Rage began to burn in Lily, remembering the anguish she'd felt when his letters had simply ceased. How could he speak about it so casually? She tugged her hands free from his warming grasp.

"I knew you weren't *alive* in Venezuela, Saige." He flinched as hard as when she struck him.

Folding her arms, Lily tucked her hands safely out of his reach. "I believed the Venezuelan government wouldn't hide you from me. But human rights violations in South America aren't a big secret. I knew you might have died somehow, been tortured and killed and your body hidden. And I'd never know. And your parents would never know. Your mother. Do you have any idea what she—"

"All right!" Saige yelled. His fists on the counter had turned white. "It was stupid, *I* was stupid. Stupider than you think. I hurt everyone.

Believe me, I know that." He shoved his fingers roughly through his hair. "I've lived with it all this time, lived with nothing else. Just the days passing, and longing and praying for the chance to explain to all of you. But doubting I'd ever get it."

"You're right," Lily said, chastened. "This is not time for recriminations. I just want...*need* to know."

"Need?" Saige sounded suspicious. "For your paper?"

"No." Lily glared at him. "So I won't have to read it in the paper. Pen's going to interview you."

"The hell he is!"

"You'll like him, Saige."

Saige shook his head. "Not a chance. I know he came here from California with Carver. They're old prep school buddies, right? Bought the paper with his family's money."

"Don't prejudge him, Saige. The rest of the town thought that at first, too, and they've changed their minds." Lily was reminded of Pen's most recent kindness in calling her this morning.

"What does he think about you and Carver?"

Lily smiled. "He says I'm too good for Randall."

Saige nodded. "He's right about that."

Talk of Pen and the newspaper had softened the tensions for both of them. Saige leaned against the sink, his arms crossed. He met her eyes. "I'll tell you what I can."

"What you *can*? Why—"

"Please, Blue, just listen," Saige said, his voice quiet but fiercely insistent. "After, you can yell or cry or hit me again if you want. But listen first." He straightened. "I was in a café in Caracas, in the center of the city, just watching the people and the traffic. It's so different from here...so bustling. So *many* cars. So far from Montana." He shot her a quick glance. "I was really missing you a lot."

"You said that just in time."

"Without you I didn't have...an anchor." Saige rubbed his fingers across his brow. "It's hard to explain how...detached I felt. And then this guy joined me, another American. He could tell I was American. We sort of stick out down there. Anyway, he was a reporter for, um, for a big city paper. We got to talking about airplanes."

"Airplanes?"

Saige nodded. "I realized later he steered the conversation that way on purpose. When he learned I had a pilot's license, he got all excited. Said he had this—" Saige grimaced so hard a muscle jumped in his cheek "—tip." Bitterness hardened the word. "He'd heard—" His voice cracked.

The rage and hurt in his voice twisted Lily's heart. "Saige," she asked, "do you want me to come another time?"

He ignored her question. "I don't even know how he heard." He looked older than he had last night, decades older. "Seven years of my life, and I don't even know how it started. Journalists!" From his lips, the word sounded like an oath. "And their sources."

His disgust made her cringe. "I'm a journalist now, Saige."

He looked at her oddly, as if he couldn't quite bring her into focus, then shook his head. "Not like this guy. Ambition made him . . . foolhardy. More than that. Nearly crazed, I think, looking back. And stupid."

Saige paused, breathing as hard as if he'd run a race. His gaze moved restlessly over the room and lighted on the coffeepot. With surprisingly steady hands, he filled two mugs and put one in front of her. Neither of them took a sip.

When he spoke again, his tone had turned cold as a tractor seat in winter. Lily shivered hearing him. "I left Caracas with him."

"Just like that?" Lily exclaimed. "You went with a stranger? A crazy, stupid stranger? Why, Saige, *why*?"

"He didn't seem so crazy at first," Saige said. "And it seemed . . ." He shook his head and shrugged.

Then Lily knew, she knew the whole thing, the reason he'd gone. "Exciting."

"Very." Saige put his cup down.

"An adventure." Lily spat the word as if it was an accusation. "The adventure of a lifetime, the one you'd always waited for."

Saige didn't deny it. He paced the length of the kitchen and back. "This isn't easy for me to tell, Blue. I've gone over it and over it in my mind, you can't imagine how often. Every time I thought about it, I tried to change the ending. But it wouldn't change."

When he reached for her hand this time, she let him take it. His fingers were cold, his grip so tight it hurt.

"That Sunday afternoon, we just took off, filed no flight plans with anyone, told no one our destination. I piloted, he navigated . . . following his *tip*." Saige's voice shook with anger and something else. A bit of fear? He paused to pull in several deep breaths. "We didn't make it. It all went wrong."

His eyes met hers, begging for understanding, longing for forgiveness with an intensity that hurt her to see. "I've thought of you every minute since, Blue. Every second, awake or asleep, I thought of you, dreamed of you, *hurt* to come back to you. But I had no choice. I made my choice when I climbed in that plane."

Lily continued to stare at him, waiting to hear the rest. When Saige remained silent, she realized he didn't mean to tell her anything more. A rage began to burn in her, so hot it nearly consumed her power to speak.

"That's it?" she said in a strangled voice. "Just that? You flew off into nowhere but you still love me?" She waved her hand, her movements so jerky she knocked her coffee mug aside, spilling half the contents. "Where did you go? What went wrong? Why couldn't you at least drop me a line?"

Her body shook so hard, she couldn't stay seated. When she stood, her knees trembled as if they would drop her. She clutched the counter for support. Saige came toward her, arms out, as if he meant to steady her, but she slapped his hands and spun away.

"Blue, please. I *can't* tell you any more. It's not over." He sounded tormented. "But it's over for me, for us. We have to let it go. It's the only way." He stretched out his hand in appeal. "You've got to trust me."

"Trust you?" Lily made a sound halfway between a laugh and a sob. "You're more insane than that reporter. How can I ever trust you again? If you trusted *me*, you'd tell me everything."

Saige looked haunted. "God, Blue, what difference does it make where I went? What I did? Do you think I didn't try everything I could to communicate with you? If I was anywhere I could have left and come home to you, don't you think I'd have done it? I'm here, alive. Those other years are gone. We only have now. We can't throw away any more time."

Lily stared at his gray-green eyes, her heart pounding uncomfortably hard. "Throw away more time?'' It took all of her will not to scream the words at him.

Though she had no doubt the anguish in his voice was real, the pain he felt as deep as hers, his love for her as fervent as he claimed, still she wanted to slap him again, to kick his shins, to scream every obscenity she'd ever heard.

Yesterday Saige's skin had been tinged with gray, but a day in the Montana sun had already put color in his handsome face. Whatever he'd lived through the past seven years, it had not destroyed his irrepressible spirit.

Hers felt as if a buffalo stampede had trampled it into the earth.

''You think you can just walk back into my life the way you walked out of it? With no explanation? No... compassion for the horror I lived through? Just, 'trust me?''' Her voice rose, becoming nearly a shriek. ''Dear Lord, Saige, do you have any idea what you did to me?''

Saige's whole body turned rigid as she shouted. ''No compassion?'' An answering anger turned his neck ruddy. ''I know how agonizing the years must have been for you—believe me—I understand the cruelty of not knowing.'' He clenched and unclenched his fists, making the muscles in his forearms stand out. ''I understand all too well. You're right, *I* knew I was alive, and I couldn't tell you. That tortured me constantly. But I didn't know anything else, Blue. Not another single damn thing. Except that it was all my fault.''

"That you got right." Lily backed away from him, putting the oak stool between them. "You did this to yourself. To all of us."

"Do you think that made it easier?" He knocked the stool aside. "I didn't know if my mother was alive, if Dad recovered from his surgery. *You* knew that. *You* knew what was happening to the ranch, to our friends, to you. God damn it, Blue, you knew whether you had a child growing inside you. Mine, I hoped . . . maybe another man's." He grabbed her shoulders. "I'm not the one who found a new career and got myself engaged to someone else, *Mrs*. Alcxander."

Lily felt as if he'd stuck a knife in her heart. "How dare you?" she cried, pounding on his chest. "What should I have done? Stayed at the ranch, burning a candle beside our cold, empty bed, withering away to nothing?"

Saige did nothing to defend himself from her flailing fists. "Blue, God, I'm sorry. I didn't mean that. I just hate the thought of that jerk anywhere near you." His grip gentled and he massaged her upper arms. "Why was the bed empty? You didn't move out right away, did you?"

"I couldn't sleep there anymore, not without you." Lily longed for the icy numbness she'd trained herself to feel in those early days of Saige's disappearance. "At first, I sat up all night on the couch. Then, when I knew it wouldn't be over soon, I tried to go back to our bed. I couldn't get in it. I slept on the floor. Grace found me one night and made me move to the guest room."

She bit down hard on her lip, trying to force the tears inside. It didn't work. "Day after day...I...so many days...I just sat there and stared at our bed...remembering...praying you weren't suffering as much as I."

Saige swore in some language Lily didn't recognize and pulled her to him. She couldn't fight him, she'd cried so many times without him, wanting so desperately to cry on his chest, in his arms, she couldn't stop herself now. Lifting her, he carried her to the old armchair by the wood stove and held her in his lap while she sobbed herself out.

His hands moved soothingly over her back, down her arms, through her hair, as he told her again and again, "I love you, Blue. It's over now. It's all right. I'll never leave you again. I love you."

When at last she could sit up and blow her nose, she felt totally drained of emotion. Love, hate, fear, anger: she'd spent them all. "Have you told Grace and Warren?" she asked dully.

Saige nodded. "I called them. I wanted to tell them in person, especially Dad. All these years he's been afraid that I left because of our bickering over the ranch that last year. But making them wait another day to hear seemed an added cruelty. I'll fly down to Tucson for a few days."

"Won't they come home now?"

"I hope I can talk them into it. But they think I need a little time here alone to..."

Lily nodded without looking up. "To recover."

"Not me. So *you* can recover. You may not feel as grief-stricken as when I disappeared." He put a finger under her chin and tipped up her head. "I hope you don't. But it's got to be almost as unsettling to have me suddenly turn up alive." He wiggled his eyebrows at her. "To use Dad's words, I need this time to concentrate on winning you back, Mrs. Alexander." He stroked a finger down Lily's suddenly slack jaw. "I have six weeks, I understand?"

Emotion came rushing back. "Six weeks?" Lily pushed his hand away. "The heck you do, you...cocky, egotistical—" She struggled to get out of his lap.

"Not cocky." He held her still. "I know I have no right to expect anything from you. But I can't help hoping. What do you think kept me alive for seven years? Dreams of my horse? Look in your heart." The quiet insistence in his tone frightened her. "Don't you, deep down, feel something for me? Something you might call love? Something that explains all the pain and anger you felt? You wouldn't feel that if you didn't care."

"No! Maybe." Lily stood up. "I don't know. It doesn't matter." She made a throwaway gesture with her hands. "I don't want that kind of love anymore. It hurts too much. It's too desperate and frightening and . . ."

She took a breath. "That wasn't the first time you left me, you know that. It was just the worst. You put off our marriage twice, for a year of college abroad then graduate school. You'll go again."

"For God's sake, Blue." His harsh tone made her jump. "Can't you understand I've changed? What do you think it does to a man to lose everyone and everything he loves for seven years?"

"I have no idea, Saige." Lily's voice began to tremble again, and she didn't fight it. Obviously, around Saige, she would never keep her emotions at bay for long. "You won't tell me. It doesn't sound to me like you changed much at all." She laughed shortly. "I'm the one who learned a lesson. I can only keep my heart safe if I never make the mistake of trusting you again." She twisted her fingers tightly together. "Trust is what I feel with Randall. He gives me the peace and security I never had, never could have, with you."

"You mean he's boring."

"I mean nothing of the kind!"

Saige folded his arms across his chest and leaned against the doorjamb, blocking Lily's way out. "You mean," he said, "if Randall was gone for seven years, it wouldn't hurt this much, because you don't care this much."

"No, no. I love Randall. I do. I'm going to marry him." Lily struggled internally with the defensiveness Saige was making her feel. "He's a wonderful man and I know what our life will be like and our children will have every benefit." She shook a finger at him. "You didn't even want children."

"I wanted children, just not so soon." Saige grabbed her extended hand and, despite her token resistance, pulled her into his arms. "I wished every hour of every day of those seven years that I'd left you with a child. You can't possibly want children more than I do." His strong right hand massaged the back of her skull, tipping her face toward his. "But the soonest I can see having one is nine months." His mouth came closer. "Want to start . . . now?" His lips teased back and forth over hers.

His mouth covered hers, demanding entry. Lily remembered the other emotion that never seemed spent with Saige—passion. She had no defenses. He was her husband, he knew how to make her want him. When she squirmed to get away, the iron band of his arm low on her spine held her tight against him, making her ache with awareness of how much he wanted her. Desire caromed through her, shooting along every nerve, swamping her reason. Lily struggled to remember why she was so mad at him. Hazily she pictured their nearby marriage bed. Weakness hit her knees.

"No," she gasped, pulling out of his embrace. "No!"

"Okay, Blue, okay." Saige's voice sounded rough with desire but tender, too, with understanding and shared pain. "I didn't mean to...push you. I love you and when I touch you..." He shut his eyes, shuddering and rubbing his fingers hard across his forehead. "I never thought I would again. I can't help..." His lids lifted and his sudden gaze seemed to penetrate her soul. "You'll never understand how much I want you...how much I love you."

"I can't, Saige," she said, wrapping her arms around her middle. "I can't make love to you when I'm engaged to another man."

All desire faded from Saige's expression. His face and body looked rigid and cold as granite. "Really?" His voice had turned to stone, too. "And how do you feel about going to bed with...your fiancé when you're married to another man?"

Though his gaze seemed pointed in her direction, Lily could tell he saw nothing. Saige looked only inward as he waited for her answer. Instinctively she knew he was thinking of his pet name for her, True Blue.

Their friends and family thought the name came from her startlingly blue eyes. Only she and Saige knew it referred to her unwavering love for her husband—a love begun in kindergarten when he rescued her from playground bullies, nurtured silently through childhood, acknowledged in adolescence and strengthened throughout adulthood. At least until now.

As Saige continued to stare blindly at her, Lily knew lying would be the kindest thing she could do for him. It would make him understand he'd already lost her, lost her years ago. A good lie now would save them both more misery.

But she had never lied to Saige and doubted she could pull off an out-and-out falsehood. "I don't have to answer that," she said, not looking directly at him. "You'll just have to *trust* me. After all, you apparently have no intention of revealing how many beds *you've* occupied the last seven years. Perhaps one day we'll decide to exchange that sort of information with each other. But it seems unlikely."

Saige's hard expression froze in place, and his eyes turned to chips of gray-green frost. Lily's stomach hurt, knowing what she'd made him believe.

Wishing she had learned to hide her emotions as well as Saige, she stood ramrod straight, biting the inside of her lip. "It wouldn't change anything anyway, Saige."

Her voice sounded strong and sure—and as if it came from someone else. It made her realize how much she had longed to hear Saige say something that *would* have made her believe he'd changed. But deep down she'd known he wouldn't. He never would.

"You'll never grow up. Look at you, coming home unannounced, without a word of explanation or warning, expecting everything simply to go back to the way you left it seven years ago. With adults, Saige, trust goes two ways."

"Lily," he bit out. He sounded angry. And disappointed. And it hurt, she couldn't believe how much, that he stopped calling her Blue—because she'd crushed his hope that she'd remained true. "I learned a lot in those lost years. I want the same things as you—home, family, peace and security. I love you."

Lily backed away, holding out a hand to ward him off. "Deep Water looks nice to you now because it's different. But what about a year from now when the ranch starts to feel confining again?"

"Confining?" Saige roared, slamming a fist against the door frame. "Working outdoors with a view of the mountains I've missed for seven years—*confining*?"

"Perhaps I chose the wrong word," Lily said. "Deep Water will certainly seem ordinary to you again some day. What if you have a child the next time you decide to take off seeking adventure? If loving me was enough for you, Saige, you'd never have left." She straightened her shoulders. "You and I can be divorced in three weeks."

"I'll fight the divorce, Lily." He slashed his palm angrily through the air. "It'll take a hell of a lot longer than three weeks. You may have to postpone your big society wedding.''

''Oh, no, Saige, we can't,'' Lily said, frustrated. ''Kokie's already sent out the invitations.''

''Do you think I give a damn?'' Saige grabbed her shoulders as if he meant to shake her. His fingers bit into her flesh as he stopped himself. ''I don't care if you've invited the president and the pope and half the population of California. I'll fight for you with everything I've got. I won't give you up.''

''You'll have to, Saige.'' Shrugging free of his grasp, Lily walked to the door. ''What we had is over. I'm going to marry Randall.''

CHAPTER FOUR

LILY parked her car on the county road and walked through Elly Wren's chicken yard to reach the hay field. In the shade of a big cottonwood tree, she leaned on the jackleg fence and watched Saige.

He was pulling some kind of plow behind Warren's old tractor. Lily was surprised it even ran anymore. Warren had bought a newer one, grumbling loudly about the ridiculous prices of farm equipment and their ridiculous accessories, like the air-conditioned cab.

But Saige had revived the old machine and sat the seat, as ranchers had for generations, exposed to the sun. Obviously he'd meant what he said about not wanting to feel confined. Wherever he'd been, he must have missed the publicity about ultraviolet rays, for he wore no shirt.

Despite the familiar tan Saige was rapidly acquiring, Lily wondered if she'd have recognized him from the back. Though she'd no longer call him painfully thin, she could easily see the vertebrae down his spine. Still . . . she studied him, remembering the way he'd felt in her arms that night in Randall's office. He'd put on several pounds.

Lily shook off the memory. She hadn't come to ogle her soon-to-be-ex-husband's body. Saige brought the tractor to a halt and sat facing away from her, surveying his work. Lily slipped through the fence and walked toward him. He didn't turn. When she reached the tractor, she knocked with her fist against the wheel housing as if knocking on a door.

At the first clang, Saige let out a shout and leaped off the tractor, disappearing behind the other side. Startled, Lily ran around the vehicle and found him leaning against it, breathing hard, his arms crossed tightly over his chest. When he saw her, he spun away.

He looked so vulnerable, Lily hurt for him. She put a hand on his bony back and felt the shaking he was obviously trying to control. "Saige?"

He didn't respond.

"What's wrong, Saige?" she asked. "What happened?"

He tried to shake her off.

She didn't move her hand. "Saige, tell me what—"

He shook his head fiercely, remaining stonily silent. Even from behind she could see stubborn resolution in the set of his neck and shoulders. She *might* get Saige to answer if she demanded to know as his wife, but even that appeared unlikely, and besides, Lily was unwilling to make that claim.

His skin felt hot beneath her fingers. "This isn't safe, you know, staying out in the sun this way without a shirt. You're starting to burn."

"I never burn." At least he was talking.

"You never used to. The sun's worse now. It's the hole in the ozone. You probably haven't—"

"I've heard," he muttered.

Lily moved her fingers and pinched the pinkest place on his back.

"Ouch!" Saige jerked away from her.

"You see?" she said. "You *are* burning. You ought to wear a sunscreen. At least fifteen SP—"

"What are you doing, Lily?" Saige whirled on her. "Nagging?" His lips quirked. "Only a wife is granted that privilege." With a halfhearted leer, he stepped toward her. "Want to sample another wifely privilege?"

He'd recovered fast. Too fast for Lily to believe him. Saige simply wanted to change the subject. But, real or forced, she wasn't ready for another confrontation like this, especially in clear view of the county road with many lumber mill employees driving home from work. She put a hand out to keep Saige away, but he took it and pressed it against his chest.

Lily pinched him again, harder.

"Yeow, woman!" he cried, jumping back.

"Keep your distance, you lecher," she said, smiling to take the edge off her words.

"Lecher? It's been seven years." A haunted look flashed through his eyes before the strained humor returned. "How many other men do you know who've gone without it for seven years?"

"No other men, Saige," she said, without thinking. "Just a woman."

Lily only realized what she'd said when she saw the intense flash of joy in Saige's eyes. Too late to do any good, she bit her tongue.

He closed his eyes. "True Blue," he whispered. He made it sound like a prayer. "I should have known."

Lily wanted to cry at the blissful relief in his voice. Guilt and regret pricked her for hurting him with her evasion last week. Yet her mind groped for words to deny or mitigate her admission. The strength of her emotions around Saige already scared her. She didn't wish to do anything to increase them.

Saige raised his lids, gazing at her as if he never wanted to look anywhere else again. The joy in his expression rapidly changed to a hunger so fierce Lily's body responded as if he'd touched her. She began to tremble.

Saige touched her cheek. "I know I should be sorry to hear that. I feel so bad for all the pain I caused you. I should feel guilty about that, too." His hand cupped her chin, forcing her to look at him. "But I can't help it, Blue—" his voice grew rough with emotion "—I'm so damn glad you waited for me."

Lily pulled her chin from his touch. "I didn't 'wait' for you. I simply couldn't bring myself to divorce a man who couldn't defend himself. I was married, after all. I don't sleep around." She gave him a piercing stare. "I won't when I'm married to Randall, either."

"You're married now," he insisted, "and not to Carver."

Lily let out a long-suffering sigh. "Saige, I didn't come out here to talk about this."

He nodded. "Talking isn't what I want to do about it, either."

She glared at him.

Saige held up both hands in surrender. "I give, I give. Why did you chase me down out here?"

"I want to ask you a favor."

"Ask," he said. "Anything you want." His gaze shifted to the distance. "Except being best man at your wedding."

"I'd like you to talk to Pen Quillan." She pushed a palm toward him before he could object. "Just let him come over and talk, Saige. Off the record if you want. He won't print the story till you say so."

"Print a story?" Saige said, incredulous. "Do you think I'd tell him anything I won't tell you?"

Lily held her ground. "I think it would be a good idea."

Saige narrowed his eyes. "Quillan put you up to this?"

"No." Lily chewed her lower lip. "He just told me how you . . . greeted him when he tried to interview you the other day."

"Greeted?" Saige laughed shortly. "I admit I wasn't very welcoming. But he retreated without a backside full of buckshot, didn't he? Why do you care so much? Just want a big scoop for your paper?"

"No." Lily wondered how much to explain. "I don't really care if you ever go on the record with Pen. I just think you need . . . no matter what you hold back . . . you need someone to talk to here. You'll like Pen."

"Lily, I have someone to talk to here. I've been talking to her since I was fifteen. She's my wife."

Lily turned and began walking toward her car.

"Wait, Blue!"

She faced him. He looked frustrated but not very remorseful.

"Look at it from my side. I didn't come home to be Deep Water's latest novelty. I need privacy. I need—"

"You need to heal, Saige, to recover from—" she waved her hand at the tractor "—whatever makes you jump off tractor seats and refuse to answer my questions."

"I can't, Blue." His voice rang with pained conviction. "I told you—"

"I know, Saige," Lily interrupted. "That's why you need a friend. I want to be your friend, but you won't let me. Every time I try to talk, you try to make love."

"I love you, damn it. What do you expect me to do?"

"I expect you to do what's best for yourself. And—" she hesitated "—for me."

"For you? You know I'd do anything for *you*."

He moved forward, but Lily stepped away, keeping space between them. Looking at him, she felt the disquieting tug at her heart that had plagued her all week. Taking sunglasses from her pocket, she slipped them on to cover any sheen that might show in her eyes.

"What do you think I've lived through the last seven years?" she asked. "Just pain of loss? Don't be silly. I'm not that shallow. I know I let you down, too."

"Let me down? Never! In your whole life, you have *never* let me down."

Lily ignored him. "When you disappeared, ever since, I kept worrying—no, dreading that whatever had happened to you wouldn't have happened if only I'd gone to South America with you, as you asked."

Saige swore viciously. "Don't, Blue. Don't say that."

He closed the distance between them. Lily ran her thumb around the tiny indentation on her ring finger where her wedding ring had remained for so long. Though she refused to wear the huge diamond ring Randall had given her while she was still legally married, she'd removed her wedding ring after Randall announced their engagement. For months, she'd fiddled with the empty space but had finally grown accustomed to the feeling. Until last week when Saige's gaze had rested there with such intensity.

"When I heard your story, I knew—" Lily swallowed, staring at Saige's naked chest.

"Stop it!" Saige commanded. Before she could duck, he reached for her sunglasses and removed them, studying her eyes intently. With his knuckle, he wiped away a tear. "Please don't do this. None of it was your fault."

"Do you expect me to believe that if I'd been there with you in the café, you'd still have gone through with this insanity?" She gazed at him through the blur in her eyes.

His sunburned chest expanded as he pulled in a long breath. "No. I wouldn't have left you." Lily heard a crack as his grip on her sunglasses tightened. "But that means nothing! It doesn't make it your fault. You aren't to blame." He held the sunglasses toward her, folding her fingers around them. "Don't say that again. Ever. Don't think it." He grabbed her shoulders and gave her a shake. "Do you understand? Don't!"

"It's too late to care about blame," Lily agreed. "But I have to know you're . . . better so I can go on with my life."

Saige put his hands on his hips. "I don't want you to go on, if you mean marrying that—preppie."

"You can't stop me, Saige, you can only make me miserable." She looked up from the wide silver belt buckle at his waist. "I didn't think you wanted to do that."

"No, that's the last thing I want." He ran a hand down his face as if trying to hide the tumult of emotions he couldn't keep from his expression. "All right. For you, I'll see your boss. But you..." He pointed at her and his hand shook. When he noticed, he quickly stuffed his fists into the pockets of his jeans. "You bring him out to the ranch tonight and introduce him. I don't want strangers in my life right now."

"About seven?"

Saige nodded without enthusiasm before climbing onto the tractor.

Feeling unutterably strange, Lily knocked on the door of the house she considered her own. Yet it was Saige's now and, unlike the day after the fourth, he had not come out on the porch to meet her.

Turning, she gazed behind her down the ranch road. She'd arrived late, hoping she wouldn't have to be alone with Saige. But Pen's car hadn't turned in yet.

"Lily?" Saige opened the door, glancing over her shoulder. "Where's your pal?"

"He's bringing his own car, in case we, um..."
Lily looked hesitantly at Saige's questioning eyes.
"I thought he should stay alone to talk to you,
Saige. It might be easier for you."

"Or harder." He took her hand. "I can say
anything I'm going to say in front of you."

"Not everything."

He flicked up a brow. "Like what?"

"Oh, like—" Lily smiled at him "—what's the
matter with that darn fool woman who used to
be my wife?"

Saige's chuckle sounded slightly forced.
"Maybe." He shot her a glance. "And you still
are my—"

"Don't, Saige." She gave an exasperated sigh.
"I want to go on being your friend. But we can't
if you don't stop... that."

"That?" Still holding her hand, he turned the
palm up and traced her life line. "You mean reminding you the commitment we made lasts a
lifetime? As in, for better or worse, until—"

Lily pulled her hand away. "It used to last a
lifetime, Saige. Now those commitments only last
till the love wears out. Ours wore out years ago."

"Mine didn't."

Lily studied the floorboards of the porch.
"Mine did."

He was silent a moment. "Want some iced
tea?" He opened the screen door for her.

Lily flicked an anxious glance at the dim interior, remembering the kiss that had ended their

last conversation inside. "Let's wait out here on the porch."

Saige shrugged. "Sure."

From old habit she'd thought long eradicated, Lily walked over to the porch swing and sat on one side. Saige joined her. Sitting in the opposite corner, he pushed the swing gently with his toe against the porch.

A companionable silence fell over them, sweeping the tensions out of Lily's body. She relaxed, remembering other nights in the swing. She loved it here on the ranch, loved the smell of new-cut hay, horse and saddle leather, loved this porch, the swing, sitting here with—

"What were you doing this afternoon?" Lily asked abruptly, changing the direction of her thoughts. "With the tractor, I mean," she added hurriedly, not wanting him to think she was again prying into his frightened reaction to her arrival.

Saige's eyes glowed with humor. "Silence never used to bother you when we watched sunsets out here together."

Pushing harder with his toe against the boards, he stretched an arm out along the back of the swing. His hand didn't quite touch her shoulder, though it could have. She could feel the heat from his arm against her skin.

She was glad, she told herself, *relieved* he hadn't touched her. She couldn't bear more tormenting physical contacts that ended only in frustration for both of them. That's why she had asked to wait outside for Pen, wasn't it? No, this sudden feeling of something shriveling inside her—that was relief, not disappointment.

"It's not the silence."

"No?" Saige's voice thickened with suppressed laughter. "You lie as well as you drink, Blue."

"Please," she said, shocked at the begging note in her voice.

"Sorry, love," he said, all hint of teasing gone. "It's just hard not to remember."

"I know," she said, speaking firmly and meeting his eyes with a steady gaze. "But I don't want to remember. I want to go forward."

Hurt lasted only a second on Saige's face. "Right," he said. "I was leveling the field this afternoon. Dad leased most of the ranch to that young couple from the Ruby Valley, but not all of it. Besides the house, he also held back those sections down by Bent Creek because they need to be flood irrigated. Told the lawyer, your fiancé, flood irrigating was a lost art."

Lily nodded. "I've heard him say that. He used to say it to you."

"Yeah." Saige's lips tilted. "Trying to convince me I ought to learn." He gave the swing another push. "But he was right—the skill's lost. I'm putting in a sprinkler system down there, a wheel line. We never lose the water out of Bent Creek, even in dry summers. And I understand the summers here have been drier than usual since

I... Lily?'' His humor returned as he gazed at her open-jawed stare.

She swallowed, closing her mouth. ''I... think that's a good idea, Saige.''

''I'll get the ranch back in January, and I'm looking for a replacement herd, a few hundred head anyway. I'll need to get at least two cuttings from—''

Rising abruptly, Lily walked toward the steps. She could no longer sit on this swing with a man who sounded like a rancher planning to stay in Deep Water.

She wrapped her hands around the porch railing and stood gazing out over the ranch. She wouldn't come here again. It was too seductive. It made her heart want too much to believe him— when her mind knew she didn't. Ranching was a novelty now. Next year, maybe the year after, it would once again seem the prison he'd always called it growing up.

Saige's footsteps approached her from behind. ''I knew what upset you last time you were here.'' His voice was gentle, laughing, though not laughing at her. ''I know what upset you this afternoon. But I'm damned if I can figure out what upsets you about a wheel line.''

He put his hands on her waist but exerted no pressure when she stepped out of his grasp. ''What happened this afternoon?'' she asked. ''When you jumped off the tractor? What scared you?''

"No."

She turned. He didn't look scared now, just resolute.

He pushed the hair off his brow, hair that had already lightened from his week in the sun. "I know what you were thinking when we sat on the swing. I was remembering, too. No matter what happens between us now, Blue, we have a lot of shared memories, good memories." His brows lowered. "You don't want my other memories. Particularly since you don't want me."

"I want..." Lily stopped. She *didn't* want him, did she? Saige had expressed it in an especially harsh way, but he'd only spoken the truth. "You're right."

Noise from the road took their attention. Lily felt almost light-headed with relief at the sight of Pen's car speeding up the ranch road in a cloud of dust. She kept her gaze on it until he pulled into the yard and climbed out.

"Pen," she called, waving as if they hadn't seen each other in weeks.

Pen gave her a curious look as he mounted the steps to the porch. "Lil."

"Pen, this is my hus—" She couldn't get the word out. "Saige Alexander, Pen Quillan." She completed the introductions in a flat tone.

"I appreciate your agreeing to see me, Saige," Pen said. "I doubt this sort of thing is easy for you."

"I don't know that it's going to be hard," Saige countered. "I haven't agreed to anything yet. In fact, let's get that clear right now. Everything I say from this moment on is off the record. Are we understood?"

Pen nodded. "If you say so."

"I do."

Lily watched the two men, shaking her head in disbelief. Saige's voice hadn't sounded so firm and strong since he'd come home. He hadn't exposed a flicker of the fear and hesitation she heard every time he spoke to her. Even Pen sounded different. Less open, more demanding.

"Men!" Lily said. "I'll leave you two alone to play this male dominance game. Maybe if you stay two weeks or two years, Pen, you'll get a decent interview. Good luck!"

Without a backward glance, she ran down the steps and jumped into her car. As she pulled out of the ranch yard, knowing it might be the last time she'd ever see her old home, Lily's heart ached as if it would split. She couldn't come here again, she knew that. And next time discontent overcame Saige, Warren would sell the place.

Lily told herself she didn't care. Hadn't she urged Warren to sell the first winter he spent in Arizona? Her grip tightened on the steering wheel as she bumped over the cattle guard. The ranch held only pain, she'd argued, for all who loved Saige. That was still true, but it was a different kind of pain now. One she couldn't understand.

Saige was alive, physically unharmed. She was going to marry a man who loved her and would never leave her. Why did she hurt at all?

Holding a white bag from the lunch counter on her lap, Lily sat bleary-eyed on the stool in the back of the pharmacy waiting for her father, Dana Harmony, to get off the phone and share lunch with her.

"Not urgent," he said to her as he hung up. Then he took another long look at her. "Something urgent with you, baby? You don't look so good."

Lily gave him a wan smile. "Thanks, Dad. That's the kind of compliment a girl likes to hear from her father."

Dana didn't laugh. "It's Saige of course."

"I don't know. I mean, yes. I guess." She swallowed hard at the lump in her throat. The lump had been there most of the night as she tossed and turned, all of the morning as she kept glancing up to catch Pen's sympathetic looks. "Last night Pen went to see him. Saige finally agreed to talk to him. Off the record, of course." Lily clamped her jaw, then unclamped it. "Maybe he can tell another man all the things he won't tell me."

"Is that what hurts you, baby?" Dana asked.

Lily shook her head. "No, I—"

"Don't let it," Dana said. "Saige may never tell us all he went through. He feels too much guilt for hurting us all. He certainly doesn't want the whole town talking about it." He took the bag from her fingers and pulled out the sandwich. "Mind if we eat?" He handed her the pasta salad. "I only have half an hour."

Lily sighed, knowing he wanted her to come to the point. "When I was out at the ranch last night, Dad, I loved it. We sat on the swing and I kept thinking about all those other times on the swing when I used to dream about sitting there as we got old and having a bunch of kids running around and later grandkids and..." She stared at the plastic fork in her hand. "Then I'd look up and remember who I was sitting with. Saige! He won't stay here. You know he won't. From the time he was a little kid, he felt trapped on the ranch."

Dana spoke quietly. "He may not feel that way anymore."

She looked up quickly. "Did he tell you that? Dad, did he tell *you* where—"

"No, not a word." Dana shook his head. "Just said how sorry he is he hurt us all. Especially you."

Lily sighed. "I'm sorry, too." She opened the container of salad and nearly gagged at the smell of olive oil and garlic. She slapped the lid back on. "You know what it did to me when he left. I can't make those memories go away. Only now... I'm so mixed up."

"Anyone would be," Dana said. "Maybe you should take it easy for awhile. Wait and see how you feel...whether Saige means to stay this time."

"Wait? How long? Another seven years?" Lily threw the salad into the wastebasket. "Dad, I want to have children."

"I know, Lily. Anyone who's ever seen you around babies knows how much you want one of your own."

"My own and my husband's," she said adamantly. "I want the man I love to stay around and help raise our children."

Dana regarded her a moment while he chewed a bite of corned beef and Swiss. "Is that all you feel for Randall? That he'll be a good father because he wants to stay in Deep Water?"

"Oh, Dad, you know it's more than that," Lily protested. "If it wasn't for Randall, I'd still be hiding out at the ranch, probably a vegetable by now. Pen would never have hired me if Randall hadn't twisted his arm. I'd never have moved to town. He pushed me some, at least at first, but it didn't really feel like pushing. Everything he did was always for my sake." She met her father's questioning gaze. "I owe him a lot."

"Owe's one thing," Dana said. "But do you love him?"

"Yes!" Lily got off the stool and began to prowl the room. "I know you're not as comfortable with him as you were with Saige, Dad, but—"

Dana made a dismissive noise. "That doesn't matter, Lily. You like Grace better than Kokie, too. So what? You and Randall are what count. Parents are...peripheral. Don't worry about us."

"Thanks." Lily gave him a tremulous smile. "I don't know if Grace will ever forgive me for marrying Randall now that Saige has come back."

She ran her fingers absently over the bottles of pills and medications on the shelves. After years of scoldings and the occasional swat from Dana, she knew better than to pick any up. "I want to do the right thing, but I don't know what it is. Tell me, Dad."

"You're the only one who can answer that, Lily." Dana came up behind her and stilled her wandering fingers. "Do you still love Saige?"

"I..." Lily looked at her father's hands on hers. "I don't know. I'm not sure I can feel anything that intense anymore—the way I *used* to love Saige, I mean. I'll never forget that feeling. I'd look at him in class, or on a horse, or coming in cold from night calving, or across the table at breakfast, and I'd feel so full of love I almost couldn't breathe."

"He used to look at you that way, too," Dana said. "Everyone could see it." He paused. "Do you love Randall that way?"

"No, I don't," Lily said without hesitation. "I don't want to." She took a shuddery breath. "I never want to have that much feeling in me again for anyone. Not for Saige, not for Randall...not anyone! It's too...painful and...scary. I remember it, but I don't feel it anymore."

"Don't or won't?"

"What does it matter? The feeling's gone."

Dana pulled Lily over to the stool. He touched the skin beneath her eyes. "Then why the dark circles? If you've made up your mind, what's the problem?"

Tears stung Lily's lids. "He won't tell me anything, but he seems so...hurt. I just can't bear adding more pain to whatever he's suffered already."

Dana pulled a tissue from a box on the counter and offered it to her, but she pushed it away. "You can't erase the last seven years, baby, not for Saige, not for yourself. You spent that time building a barrier inside you around the feelings you used to have for him. A barrier so thick, no one can ever get through it to hurt you like that again. You had to. It took you a long time."

"Randall helped." She gulped for the hundredth time at the ache in her throat.

"I know he did. Saige didn't have anyone helping him get over you, and he didn't want to. All he had was his dream that he'd come back to you one day and everything would be the same."

"It can't be the same!" Lily cried. "How can he expect me to—"

Dana held up a palm. "He doesn't expect anything. That was just his dream. It kept him going when he had nothing else. Now he'll have to go on with his life, just as you did with yours. But he won't be able to let go of the dream overnight." He stroked her hair. "Look how long it took you."

Lily took the proffered tissue and blew her nose. "I have to know he's healing, Dad, that he'll...be whole again one day, or I'll always feel guilty with Randall. I won't be able to enjoy our happiness."

Dana frowned and turned away so she couldn't see his eyes. "If he heals into the old Saige, it may mean..."

"He'll take off again," Lily said. "No one knows that better than me. I don't have a doubt in my mind that's what he'll do. But if it means he's happy, I won't mind. At least this time he'll tell us where he plans to go."

"I don't think he'll discuss his plans with you and Randall," Dana said dryly.

"Of course not," she agreed. "But he'll tell you and Grace and Warren. I mean, at least I won't be lying awake terrified that some insane adventure he couldn't resist has gotten him killed or—" heat rushed into her cheeks "—wondering who he's sharing his bed with at night."

Dana cocked a brow. "If you're still worrying about Saige's bed partners, Lillabeth, you probably haven't resolved all your feelings for the man. Maybe you should delay your wedding until you—"

"Delay my wedding?" Lily jumped up. "I can't hurt Randall that way."

"You'll hurt him a lot more if you marry him just because he's helpful and safe, when you're still in love with another man."

"I am *not* still in love with Saige!" Lily insisted. "Not the way you mean." She doubled up her fists but had nowhere to pound them that wouldn't knock over pill bottles. Besides, her feelings about Saige weren't really clear enough to make her comfortable with such an emphatic gesture. She dropped her hands to her lap. "Most of what I remember about loving Saige is pain and worry—not my idea of happiness. Randall and I have set a date, and I mean to keep it."

Dana covered her fists with his big hands. "Okay, baby. If you're sure, I'd never try to talk you out of it." He let out a gusty sigh. "I just wish you had a woman to talk this over with. Grace has always been there for you in the past, but she can't help with this." He gave her a smile. "Neither can Kokie."

At last Lily chuckled. "No kidding. I can't imagine *anyone* having a talk like this with Kokie, even her husband." She gave her father an affectionate pat on the cheek. "I guess you're stuck, Dad. This is the trouble you get into when you try to be father *and* mother to a girl child. You should have thought of that when you decided not to get me a stepmother."

Dana didn't match Lily's lighthearted tone. "I thought about that a lot, Lily. More than you know. But after Meg..." He shrugged. "When you've found perfection in love, it's hard ever to settle for second best."

CHAPTER FIVE

OF ALL days, Lily loved her job on Thursdays best. When Pen first changed the paper from a weekly to a daily, the townsfolk had not responded with enthusiasm. It wasn't that they minded buying a paper every day, but they missed the local gossipy news that they'd read in the *Register* for seventy years.

It didn't take Pen long to realize that if he wanted to sell ads Friday through Wednesday, he'd better keep Thursday's paper just as it had always been. No news outside Deep Water, nothing more serious than the bowling league roll off.

Most weeks, someone, or several someones, dropped in after reading the Thursday edition to thank Lily for an article, or complain about her choice of Recipe of the Week, or admire her picture of their adorable grandchild, or suggest she hadn't sounded excited enough about the grand slam doubled and redoubled at the duplicate bridge club. Lily listened to the complaints almost as gladly as the compliments, since at least it meant people were reading what she wrote.

But this Thursday, all she could do was stare at her desk calendar, hearing her father's words echo around and around in her brain.

Settle for second best? Is *that* what she was doing?

In the six years since she'd met Randall and grown gradually more and more fond of him, she'd never thought of him as second best. In fact, she'd diligently avoided ever comparing him to Saige at all. What did it matter? Saige was dead.

Now she had trouble not comparing the two men. She loved, or had loved, both of them. She couldn't see Randall without thinking of Saige. Lily pushed a hand through her hair. Oh, how she wanted to go somewhere alone for a few weeks to think things over, without either man pulling at her emotions.

The door to the newspaper office slammed open hard. Lily winced. Today, she decided, she was not in the mood to listen to a lot of gripes. One look at the man framed in the open doorway and she knew exactly which article he'd come to complain about.

Saige covered the length of the small office in three long strides and halted in front of her desk. "What the hell is this, *Miss* Harmony?" He slapped the paper down on her desk blotter.

Staring up at her was the headline she'd written a few hours ago—Local Rancher To Install Wheel

Line. It wasn't a very big headline; it wasn't on the front page or even the second. In fact, it was buried in the back of the paper where the school lunch menu usually went in the winter. She'd tried to call Saige this morning to let him know she'd written it, but he hadn't answered the phone. Obviously, however, he'd found the article unerringly without her help.

Trying to gauge the extent of his anger, Lily turned her gaze to him and almost flinched. He could only look more ferocious if he put on twenty pounds. Ire showed in every line of his powerful body, in the clenched fists planted on his hips, the lowered brows and tight lips. His eyes had grown dark as thunderclouds. Perhaps hurt still lingered in them beneath the fury, but Lily couldn't see it through his narrowed lids.

Emotion flooded her: not an answering anger, or anxiety at the tirade Saige so obviously meant to deliver any moment, or even dismay at the realization that her boss would probably hear every word of this tongue-lashing through the closed door to his office. No, the emotion that rose in her and put joy in her heart was relief. Relief that Saige could overcome sorrow and guilt and hurt long enough to work up this massive annoyance with her.

It seemed so healthy, Lily couldn't help smiling. In fact, she had trouble not laughing, she felt so freed from guilt. "Oh, Saige. You look wonderful. You must have liked talking to Pen."

"Talking to Pen?" Saige roared, loud enough to make her push back in her chair. "Damn right! At least he didn't come down here and print everything I'd told him the second he left my sight."

Lily swallowed. "You didn't go off the record with me, Saige."

"Off the record? With my *wife*?" He jabbed a finger toward her. "And don't tell me again you're not my wife."

"I'm—"

"Estranged wife, then. You know damn well I didn't expect you to print everything I said to you." He raked a hand through his ever-lightening locks. "Lily, I told you I didn't come home to be Deep Water's latest gossip item."

"No, Saige," she said, fighting a stab of remorse. "But you did come home to ranch. I thought putting that in, as though you were...you know, just any other local rancher, would sort of...dispel gossip, not fan it. I mean *everyone* knows you're home. At least this way, they'll realize you came home to run the ranch and not feel like they have to ask you personally, each and every one of them."

Saige opened his mouth to respond, then shut it again, shaking his head and rolling his eyes as if he couldn't believe what she'd said. Turning aside, he grabbed the empty chair from the other desk used by the part-time secretary two mornings a week. He pulled it up to hers and slumped into it.

"I guess that makes some convoluted sense," he said. "I tell you I want privacy and you try to get it for me by advertising my every move." He placed his elbow on her desk and leaned his chin on his hand. "About as much sense as me coming in here like I want to haul you out of that desk and warm your backside—and you telling me I look wonderful."

She gave him a wry grin. "You did, Saige. You do. Last night on the swing, all the ... memories. I bet you would've sworn you'd never be angry with me again."

He flicked up a brow. "I wouldn't if you'd told me what you planned to publish this morning."

"That's the point." She turned up her palms. "I mean, it's so ... normal. I wrote a story about just one more rancher in the valley, you got mad and yelled at me. Do you know how many people yell at me every Thursday?"

Saige met her gaze with an unwavering stare. "Okay, now explain this one." He stabbed a finger at her byline beneath the story, By Lillabeth Harmony. "Tell me what that means, my True Blue love."

Lily's heart beat oddly, out of sync. "That's my name, Saige. The name I write under."

"You said you didn't divorce me because I couldn't defend myself." He looked at the paper, aiming all his hurt and confusion at her byline. "What's the difference if you cast me out of your life in print, week after week, for seven years?"

"Lots of married women write under their maiden names, Saige. And they're called Ms., not Miss." A cleansing wave of irritation swept over her. "I guess the women's movement didn't reach you wherever you were. I'll continue to write as Lillabeth Harmony after I marry Randall, too."

"I don't give a damn what you call yourself after you're married to him. Nor what you called yourself when you thought I was dead."

He stared out the window a moment, a deep frown creasing his brow. Lily wondered if he aimed his glare at Randall's office across the street, with its false Western front and hitching posts, or if his gaze had turned inward and his frown was meant for her.

"I really do understand how hard this is for you." His fingers tightened around the arms of his chair till his knuckles turned white. "But couldn't you find some way a little less blunt to announce to everyone that even alive I'm just another rancher and you're just a reporter—not the woman I love and remain married to?"

"Saige, I—"

He reached across the desk and enfolded her hand in his. "Can't you understand how this hit me when I saw it? You don't even sound angry or hurt, just indifferent."

"I'm not indifferent." His thumb tracing across her palm, following her life line, sent melting signals up her arm. "I wish I was."

"We shared more than a marriage bed, Blue."
His grip tightened on her fingers. "We shared all
that other stuff—hopes and dreams, insecurities
and frustrations, good times and bad. Remember
the time Mom caught us in the barn and you were
so embarrassed you wouldn't come to dinner for
weeks? And all those times you fell in the mud
trying to move sprinkler pipe."

Lily pulled her hand free, scared of what his
words and touch were doing to her emotions.

"And how we felt seeing New York together
from the top of the World Trade Center? And
that cockroach-infested one-room apartment in
the Village, where the kitchen was so small you
had to back into the living room to open the oven?
Do you know how hard it was to study when your
luscious backside kept popping in and out of my
sight?"

Lily's mind sped through the pictures Saige
evoked, like a video on fast forward. "Please stop
that," she begged, her voice as uneven as her
thoughts. "Please."

Saige's green eyes met hers. "We shared a
whole life together, Blue. That's why we shared
a name. Couldn't you, when you were writing
about your husband and *our* ranch, couldn't you
just once have used *our* name?"

Lily had fought tears all day. Now she quit
trying. "I tried to call you, but..." She drew a
breath that turned into a sob. "That's just the
name I use. I didn't think..."

Saige came around the desk and pulled her into his arms. "Don't cry, Blue. Don't. I don't want to make you cry."

"And I—" she sniffed "—never meant to hurt you more. I'm just so confused. You're back, but I still don't know where you've been . . . why you stayed away. Seven years have happened, Saige. They can't just go away."

"I know, I know." He stroked her back soothingly as her crying eased. "This kind of stuff'll probably keep happening to me. So many changes without enough time to absorb them all." She felt a shudder pass over him. "I just didn't expect them so publicly."

She sniffed against his shirt, taking comfort from the feel of his arms around her. "What did you say to Pen last night?"

Saige chuckled. "You haven't changed a bit, have you, woman?" Without looking up, she knew he was shaking his head at her. "You go out of your way to get me someone to talk to in private, then you want to know what we said."

Lily looked up at him, smiling tremulously. "But it helped? You liked him?"

He nodded. "I liked him a lot. It was a good idea. But it was off the record, more from you than anyone." He wiped a tear off her cheek. "Look at you. You've been hurt enough." He bent his head toward her. It seemed the most natural thing in the world that he would kiss away her tears.

A door opened behind them, and Pen cleared his throat. "I guess this is off the record, too. Right?"

Lily flushed and stepped back, out of Saige's embrace. She bumped her desk chair and plopped into it. "I'll explain to Randall," she told Pen. "He'll understand."

Pen raised his brows. "No, Lil, he won't. Better just forget it."

"I don't like to lie to Randall, Pen."

"Well, here's your chance." He gestured at her phone. "Randall's on the line for you."

She stared at the phone on her desk, surprised to see the hold light flashing. She hadn't even heard it ring. She lifted the receiver and gulped back the last of her tears. "Hello," she said.

"Lillabeth?" Randall said. "Is that you? You sound odd."

"Of course it's me, Randall."

"Yes." He hesitated a moment. "Mother asked me to call you. One of the little girls at the horse camp fell off her horse yesterday. She didn't get hurt, but she's scared to get back on." He sounded worried. "We don't want to have to send her home early."

Lily forced her mind to switch gears to Kokie's pride and joy, her City Kids Summer Horse Camp. Kokie raised money for lots of charities, but this one she funded entirely on her own.

Every summer, she brought twelve kids from California inner cities to Deep Water for a month on her dude ranch, the C Bar Three, where they learned to ride and see what living on a ranch was like. They had to help the cowboys with ranch chores, but all their expenses were paid.

"What do you want me to do, Randall?"

"She needs ... Well, the cowboys can't spend much time with just one child. She needs someone to teach her individually." A horse nickered in the background, and Lily wondered if Randall was using the phone in the barn. "Can you think of anyone, Lillabeth, who could devote a few weeks to this little girl?"

Lily couldn't help it. A broad smile stretched across her face. "Oh, can I ever," she said. "But you won't like it."

"At the moment," Randall said firmly, "what I don't like is the idea of sending this child home to San Diego after promising to keep her for a month. I'm sure her parents made plans and expect us to honor our commitment. But she can't stay here without supervision."

"I understand," Lily assured him. "And I do know someone who has a lot of free time just now, who happens to be the best horseman in the valley and who's very good at teaching frightened young girls. Do you want me to ask him?"

Not a sound came from Randall's end of the wire for a long time. "No, Lillabeth," he said finally. "I don't think I do. You're speaking of your former husband, aren't you?"

"Yes. He's right here, in fact. I could ask him now and—"

"I don't think that's a good idea at all." Randall interrupted her. "You know how much contact you have with these kids. You'd see him quite a bit."

"Well, that's bound to happen in a town this size, no matter what he does."

"Last night you were quite firm in your desire to avoid him." Randall's reproachful tone failed to hide his nervousness. "You told me in so many words how uncomfortable you felt in his presence."

"Yes, at the ranch. At . . . where we used to live together, Randall."

Lily glanced up and realized Pen and Saige had not moved from in front of her desk. Both stared at her with varying degrees of curiosity. She had a moment of sympathy for Saige's desire to avoid public discussion of his personal life.

"Dear, let's talk about this somewhere else. I'm at work. But remember, it's the little girl we need to worry about, not ourselves."

"Yes, of course." Randall sounded remorseful. "You're right. Ask him, then. For Crysta. That's her name. But warn him if he disrupts our smooth operation out here, he'll have me to answer to."

"I'll tell him," Lily said, doubting Randall's threat would strike much fear in Saige's heart. She looked at his stony expression. "If he agrees."

"What's he doing there, anyway? Pestering you?"

"He came about an article in the paper." Lily forced a chuckle. "Just as so many other readers do on Thursdays."

"Actually, my dear," Randall said, making no effort to hide his disapproval, "I have to agree with him in this instance. I thought it ill-advised to put that story in the paper the moment I saw it."

"Thanks for your support," Lily said sardonically.

"Now, now." Randall laughed. "I see I've hit a nerve. Don't worry, sweetheart, the writing was lovely."

"Glad to hear it, Randall."

He chuckled magnanimously. "Very well. Ask your horseman, and if he agrees, he might want to come right out. Crysta's pretty upset after a day of being alone while her camp mates rode. I think she ended up just doing a lot of chores." He made a kissing sound against the phone. "See you for dinner."

"Let's eat at my apartment, Randall. I want to relax."

"Mother thought we—"

"Can't you get out of it? I'm exhausted."

Randall hesitated. "Of course I can. We'll go to my house, I've got shrimp in the freezer. See you there."

Lily replaced the receiver and looked at Saige, wondering how best to broach this subject. She remembered him teaching her to ride when she was eight and he was twelve. That had not been Saige's idea, either. His mother and Lily's father had cooked up the scheme and twisted Saige's arm. But despite the fact that he'd rather have been anywhere else than teaching a "baby" to ride, he'd been gentle and careful with her and her horse.

Crysta would love him, Lily was sure, if only he'd agree to teach her. She wondered how Grace and Dana had convinced him when he was twelve.

"I have a favor to ask of you, Saige."

A brow flicked up. "You asked a favor yesterday. How many do you want? One a day?"

"You said you'd do anything I asked except..." She glanced at Pen and let that sentence remain unfinished.

"That was before your paper came out. I know better than to agree in the abstract today."

"Did Pen tell you about the City Kids Summer Horse Camp?"

When Saige shook his head, looking suspicious, she explained without mentioning Kokie's name. After all, the dude ranch didn't even adjoin Kokie's place. Saige could spend the summer there and never see her, nor she him. By the time Lily got to the part about Crysta, Saige looked more sympathetic than suspicious.

"And you want me to teach her?"

"Well, you could spend so much time with her on a one-to-one basis," Lily said. "The way you did with me. I'd never have learned to ride if you hadn't taught me. And—"

"Save the syrup, Lily," Saige said. "I'll do it. When do we start?"

"How about now?" she said. "Crysta's pretty lonely, I understand. I can tell you how to get to the ranch."

"No." Saige shook his head. "You can take me there."

"Take you there?" Lily said, gesturing at her skirt and pumps. "I can't go to the ranch like this."

"I'll wait for you to change," Saige said. "After all, I have a lot of time on my hands, remember?"

"Okay, then you can follow me in your car."

Saige shook his head again. "You ride with me. I'll bring you to town in time for you to meet Carver for your date."

Lily looked at the set of Saige's shoulders, the clamp of his jaw. Firm as they looked, neither convinced her arguing would waste her time. It was the look in those gray-green eyes that left her no doubt. She'd seen the look too often before to misunderstand its meaning. Saige wouldn't go without her, and Crysta was waiting.

"Don't waste your breath, Lil," Pen said, giving her an understanding smile.

Lily switched her glare to him, torn between exasperation and amusement. "How long have you known him, exactly?"

"Twelve hours." Pen laughed. "Long enough."

Twenty minutes later, Lily opened the passenger door of Saige's pickup, then leaped back. Firmly ensconced in the passenger seat, a large, heavily bandaged orange and gray cat spat and hissed at her, refusing to move.

"Gosh, Saige," Lily said, eyeing the cat from a safe distance. "Couldn't you afford a guard *dog*?"

"Better get in on my side," Saige said. "Invictus likes the air vent over there."

"He's welcome to it," Lily said, climbing in the driver's side and sliding under the wheel. "Where did this creature come from?"

"I found him in the barn," Saige said, "all beat up from cat fights. Had him at the vet's all morning. He'll probably lose his right eye, but Doc thinks he'll make it. So I named him Invictus—it means unconquered. Remember that poem we learned in high school?"

"From Mrs. Shaw."

"Right." Saige leaned across her lap to scratch the beast behind its ears. "He's not very nice. Nearly ate Doc's hand off. He and I have a lot in common." He shot a glance at Lily, then looked back to the road. "You know, alone, unconquered, fighting for our women."

"And beat up?" Lily asked.

Saige sighed. "Invictus and I, we got ourselves in trouble, Blue. Maybe we had it coming." He covered her hands, folded in her lap. "Don't let yourself get beat up by knowing us. Okay?"

Touched that Saige would worry about her when he felt so much pain himself, Lily refrained from pulling her hands away. "Okay," she murmured.

"I mean it, Blue." Saige gave her fingers a final squeeze. "Take care of yourself first, no matter what I say. Or Carver, for that matter. You deserve all the happiness you can get."

"I wish you'd do that, too, Saige." Lily looked out the window at the pines bordering the road as they climbed. "Look after yourself first. Find some happiness."

"I blew my chance when I went with that reporter." His voice sounded deep and husky. "But it's not too late for you."

As Saige steered the pickup around the sharp right-hand curve at the top of the draw, Lily swayed against him. Her mind swelled with memories of other times they'd climbed this road in a pickup, when privacy from her father or Saige's parents or even high school friends had been hard to find, when swaying against Saige and staying there pressed to the warmth of his muscular physique had been the main reason for coming.

Now she straightened her body away from the provocative contact with Saige's, trying not to move too close to Invictus, who growled under his breath at the rocking motion of the truck and stretched his claws toward her leg. Sitting stiffly between them, Lily folded her hands and stared straight ahead out the windshield.

Montana's second-highest mountain range loomed before them as they emerged from the draw onto the high bench. The gravel road stretched long and narrow ahead of them, a yellow slash through fields of alfalfa toward the dark green forest of the canyon where the dude ranch was situated.

Saige's hand bumped against her knee as he shifted the truck out of second. Lily looked down to see his fingers leave the gearshift and hesitate, hovering over her leg, as if he meant to give her thigh a squeeze the way he always had in the past. Memories of other drives on the bench road must have struck him, too. Lily tensed, dreading his touch and the distress it would bring her as much as she craved it.

Saige returned his hand to the wheel. "Don't worry, Blue," he said softly. "God knows, I want to, but not at the expense of your peace of mind." He chuckled. "Your virtue is safe with me, my dear." He laughed louder. "How many times did we tell your father that when we were on our way up this very road?"

Lily laughed, too. "I hope your word means more now than it did then, Saige Alexander. My virtue never felt a moment's safety alone with you."

"I don't recall ever forcing you into anything," Saige said dryly. "In fact—"

Lily elbowed him sharply in the ribs. "Try to behave like a gentleman, Saige."

Saige groaned pitifully, holding his ribs. "I'm not sure of the etiquette when doing one's estranged wife a favor and she starts reminding one of all the—" His eyes widened. "What the hell?"

Saige hit the brakes and brought the pickup to a halt. His jaw slack, he stared down the valley at circle after circle of irrigated hay fields stretching along the bench into the horizon.

"Who put that pivot system in up here?" he asked. "It must have cost a fortune."

"It's gravity feed," Lily said. "So it was only a *small* fortune."

Saige shook his head in awe. "Do you know what it's costing me to put in one wheel line on a couple hundred acres and... Look at that. It must be twelve hundred acres."

"Fifteen," Lily said.

"Whose ranch is this? It used to belong to..." He looked at her, frowning as he tried to remember. "Three or four families owned the bench, didn't they? And it was just pasture, not irrigated."

Lily nodded. "Kokie bought all three of them," she said, forgetting that she hadn't mentioned the Carver name earlier when she'd told Saige about the horse camp. "That's where the dude ranch and her summer place came from."

Saige's curious frown turned into a scowl, directed at Lily. "Kokie?" he said, very quietly. "Carver's mother?"

"Um, yes."

"*She* owns this dude ranch?" He put his arm along the back of the seat and leaned toward her. "*Kokie* wants help with her summer camp?"

"No," Lily said adamantly, feeling walled in by Saige and his man-eating cat. "A little girl named Crysta wants help."

Saige reached for the ignition and turned off the truck. "Tell me what's going on, Blue. Why does Kokie—" his lip curled as he said the name "—need three ranches for her summer entertaining?"

"She doesn't. She bought the first ranch to build her summer place. It was Tom Ingalls's place, and he sold out because he couldn't afford to operate anymore. You know how marginal it was. Kokie didn't realize until after she bought it that it couldn't begin to pay for itself."

"If all she wanted was a summer place," Saige asked, "why did she care?"

Lily shrugged. "I think it had something to do with taxes. Anyway, she bought two more ranches and turned the one closest to the forest, with access to the wilderness, into a dude ranch. The working parts of all three ranches, the pasture, the herds, the hay fields, she put in the working ranch under one manager.'' She waved down the valley. ''That's where she got all the land and all the water.''

Saige was still frowning. ''You can't just shift water rights around like that. You have to—''

''She found that out, too,'' Lily interjected. ''That's why Randall came up here the first time. To help straighten out the legal mess she was getting herself into.''

''Yeah?'' Saige growled. ''Why'd he stay?''

Lily gazed out the side window. ''Well, Kokie needed him for quite some time. He's still on retainer to all three ranches.''

''All three?'' Saige hooted. ''He stays here because he's on Mama's payroll?'' He made a rude noise.

''He has other clients, too,'' Lily said defensively.

''Didn't he have some hotshot job in California?''

Lily tightened her lips at Saige's disrespect. ''Indeed, he did, Saige.'' Her voice sounded stuffy even to her, and she tried to lighten it. ''That's the first thing I loved about Randall. He didn't want to go back to his old law firm. He loved Deep Water too much ever to leave. And he loved *me* too much to take me away from my home.''

Saige looked as if several ungentlemanly things to say crossed his mind, but he restrained himself.

Lily looked out at the view she loved. "When I came up here the first time with him, I was scared and almost sick with grief." She stared across the valley to the opposite bench where she could just see Saige's ranch—*her* ranch. "I was afraid I'd break down and cry from all the memories."

"Like today," Saige put in gently.

"Like today," Lily agreed. "Only it didn't happen, because Randall was as enthralled with the beauty as I am. You—" she poked a finger at him "—used to call these mountains prison walls. All you could think of when we came up here was what was waiting for you on the other side of them."

"Like hell," Saige said, his tone husky. "When I brought you up here, believe me, my mind was not on mountains."

Lily flushed but didn't turn away. "Randall saw at once what I loved up here. He—"

"Stop it, Lily!" A muscle jumped in Saige's cheek. "I do *not* want to hear all the reasons you love Randall. And I sure as hell don't want to do a favor for him and his mother!"

Lily waved her hand down the valley. "All that space separates the dude ranch from Kokie's place. You'll never see each other. It's Crysta who needs you."

"Ha!" Saige declared. "They just don't want to send Crysta home early. Makes 'em look bad. Why do I care if they look bad?"

"Oh, fine!" Lily said. "You and Randall, what a pair. He didn't want you up here, either. And here's this poor little girl who needs help caught between your two puffed-up male egos."

She threw up her hands, accidentally letting one get too near Invictus. With a hiss, he swatted at her, narrowly missing her wrist with his outstretched claws. Snatching her hands out of his range, she folded them in her lap.

Without taking his glare from Lily, Saige scratched Invictus behind the ears. "How old is this little girl?"

"Probably ten or so, no more than twelve."

"Poor kid," Saige muttered, turning to the wheel. "It's not her fault." He sat a moment, regarding the road. "Carver didn't want me up here, huh? Why not?"

"He thought we'd see too much of each other," Lily told him. "I spend quite a bit of time with the kids."

Saige grinned devilishly. "Say no more... Lillabeth."

Giving the ignition a twist, he yanked the truck into gear and headed up the bench.

CHAPTER SIX

WHEN Saige turned at the dude ranch, Lily directed him around back to the stable yard. Sitting on a half-log step of the grain shed was a little girl who must be Crysta. She wore baggy jeans, a cut-off T-shirt and the most suspicious look Lily had ever seen on a child.

"Poor little kid," Saige said, watching Crysta's small brown arm circle the rough-cut newel post and cling to it. "Probably thinks we're going to strap her to a horse and send her into the wilderness."

As he got out of the truck and walked toward her, Crysta, with a toss of her head, flipped the curly black bangs that hung determinedly over her right eye. Lily's view of both eyes lasted only a second before the too-long bangs flopped once again into place. Long enough to see that the look from her right eye was no less wary than that from her left.

"Who're you?" Crysta asked. " 'Nother cowboy?"

Saige cocked his head as if pondering his answer. "Used to be," he said. "I will be again—

soon as I get some cows." He put out his hand to shake. "I'm Saige Alexander."

Crysta released the post only long enough to shake Saige's hand. "My name's Crysta Johnson." She gripped the porch again. "You think you're gonna make me ride a horse—like those other cowboys?"

"Don't you like the cowboys?" Saige asked.

"They're all right," Crysta said. "But I ain't gettin' on a horse again."

Saige sat down beside her. "Who says you have to?"

Crysta pointed at Lily, who stood near the pickup, listening but not interfering. "Miss Harmony. And Mr. Carver and the great pink-haired lady."

Lily sputtered and looked at the ground, biting her lip to hold back laughter. "I never said you had to, Crysta."

"Well, Mrs. Carver does." Once again her young voice resounded with resentment at the mention of Kokie.

Saige did not trouble to hide his laughter. "Know what Mrs. Carver's friends call her?"

Crysta shook her head.

"Kokie," he said. "Sounds like a soda pop, doesn't it?"

Crysta giggled. "Yeah."

Saige slid down and leaned his elbows on the step behind him, bringing his eyes to Crysta's level. "You don't have to stay if you don't like it. You can go home whenever you want."

"Can't."

"Oh, honey, of course you can," Lily said, taking another step toward the pair. "We would never keep you here against your will."

Crysta looked at her stonily, her lower lip pushed out.

Saige put his hand on the top of Crysta's head and turned her to face him. "Did your mom and dad take a trip or something while they knew you'd be away?"

Crysta's pouting lip began to tremble. "Not my daddy."

Saige cocked his head. "So your daddy's home?"

Crysta swallowed several times before answering. "My daddy died in Desert Storm."

Saige's face crumpled with sadness. He put an arm around Crysta's shoulders. "Ah, Crysta, I'm sorry. That really sucks. It's so unfair—when so many dads got to come home."

"My mama says I should be proud."

"You should," Saige agreed. "But that doesn't mean you can't be sad, too. And mad that it seems like your dad was the only one."

At the compassion in Saige's voice, Crysta's eyes filled with tears. He gave her shoulder a gentle squeeze, and she spun around, pushing her face hard against his chest, where he held her tightly. Lily ached to offer the little girl comfort, but she didn't want to break the spell of Saige's sympathy. His voice as well as his words made it clear he felt Crysta's grief profoundly.

After a moment Crysta spoke in a mumble. "My mama told her boyfriend I was goin' away for a month. They want..." Her voice trailed off.

Saige hugged her tighter. "You and I have a lot in common, Crysta. I came home a month too soon, too."

Crysta looked up. "You did?"

"Yup." Saige lifted his gaze to Lily, and the longing in his eyes hit her like a blow. "Made someone and her boyfriend real mad, too."

Crysta looked back and forth from Saige to Lily. She seemed confused and returned her grip to the post. "I still ain't gettin' on a horse."

Saige stood and held out his hand to her. "Let's just look at some horses."

She stared at his hand. "Long as you promise you won't put me on one."

"Cross my heart." Saige made an X motion over his chest. "I won't *make* you do anything."

"She comin'?" Crysta asked, gesturing at Lily.

"I don't know." Saige grinned while pretending to consider the question. "I think she's okay. What do you think?"

Lily almost held her breath awaiting Crysta's judgment. She'd come here last Saturday with Randall to welcome the kids to the ranch, and Crysta no doubt associated her with the Carvers, whom she now clearly regarded with suspicion.

If Crysta didn't want her along, Lily would understand. But watching Saige win over the little girl was doing funny things to her heart. She didn't want them to exclude her from their circle of warmth.

"Yeah," Crysta said at last. "Miss Harmony can come."

Saige's grin faded a bit. "Let's call her Lily, okay?"

"Mrs. Carver told us—"

"Just when you're with me," Saige said. "Please?"

Something wounded in his tone made Lily squirm inside.

Crysta must have heard it, too, for she took his hand and squeezed. "Okay."

"And we'll call Mrs. Carver the pink-haired soda pop."

"Saige!" Lily said, feeling she simply had to defend Kokie's name.

Saige ignored her and headed toward the corrals with the giggling Crysta. Lily traipsed along behind the pair, who continued to hold hands. At the fence, Saige put a booted foot on the bottom rail and pointed at a smallish blood bay mare.

"If you *were* going to ride," he said, "not that I think you are, but if you were, I think you ought to ride that horse." He stretched a hand toward the mare, urging her closer with kissing sounds. "C'mon, girl. C'mon."

The horse trotted obligingly toward the group at the rail.

"Saige," Lily began.

"I ain't ridin'," Crysta said. "And I can't ride her anyway. She's Miss—she's Lily's horse."

Saige stroked the mare's muzzle. The horse put her head over the fence and nudged his chest. "I bet Lily'd let you ride her. What's her name, Blue?"

Lily opened her mouth, then shut it again. "Of course, Crysta can ride her," she said finally. "This is a special case."

"I ain't ridin' a horse!" Crysta hollered. She stepped back, glaring at Saige. "You promised."

Saige quit nuzzling the horse and turned to Crysta. "How about just patting this horse?"

She narrowed her eyes at him. "Okay. But don't start that other stuff."

"Okay. Give me your hand."

Together Saige and Crysta began patting the horse. "Tell you what. I'll ride her. You just watch." Crysta nodded slowly, eyes narrowed. "Then if it looks to you like I can control her, you can get up on her with me. I won't leave you alone on her back. Not for a second."

Crysta snatched her hand away from Saige's. "You tryin' to trick me, man?"

Saige bent his knees, bringing his eyes to Crysta's level. "Yeah," he said, grinning unrepentantly. "Is it working?"

"No!" Crysta hollered. "No way! I ain't that stupid." She stuck out her lower lip. "You promised you wouldn't make me ride."

"I meant it," Saige assured her. "I won't make you. I'll try to convince you. But you get to decide, Crysta."

Crysta pursed her lips. "You sure?"

"When I give my word, Crysta, I mean it."

She gave him a long one-eyed stare and finally nodded.

Just as Lily felt her shoulders relax, Saige hit her with his questioning look again. "What's her name, Blue?"

Lily bit her lip.

"I know," Crysta said. "We call her Scra. Her real name's somethin' like Sera Dippy."

Saige's smile started slowly, curving his lips till his teeth showed white, then spread to his eyes, making all the little lines around them crinkle with pleasure. It was the same kind of look he'd given her his first night home, after he'd kissed her in Randall's office.

"Does Carver know?" he asked.

"'Course he does," said Crysta. "He told us."

Saige raised his brows in silent question at Lily.

She couldn't seem to tear her gaze away from him. He could see inside her now, she knew that, see to something deep she'd never questioned until this moment. But the enjoyment in his eyes gave her such pleasure to see, she could not deny herself. Imperceptibly she shook her head.

Saige's smile broadened. Reaching into the pickup, he grabbed his old Stetson and offered his other hand to Crysta. Slightly dazed, Lily meandered to the grain shed and took up Crysta's place on the step. As she watched Saige and Crysta disappear into the tack room to find a saddle, she knew the little girl had lost her battle to stay off horses. No doubt Crysta would love riding before the day was out.

It was her internal battle that troubled Lily now. Why *had* she named this horse, the horse Randall had given her, Serendipity? The name held a thousand memories for her—but the memories were of Saige, not Randall.

Lily stared at Saige as he saddled and mounted her mare, but her mind's eye saw only the first Serendipity, Saige's old Welsh mountain pony, the one he'd taught Lily to ride on when she was eight years old. Naturally she'd named the mare Saige had given her as a wedding present Serendipity, too. The name meant so much to them by then. Saige said meeting Lily was the most serendipitous thing that had ever happened to him.

So why, she asked herself, had she named Randall's horse Serendipity? Here in this Carver bastion, why had she tormented herself with memories of Saige?

The creak of saddle leather brought Lily's gaze up to see Saige leaning down from Sera's back and pulling Crysta up in front of him. Smiling with almost no nervousness, Crysta put her hands over his on the reins.

Perhaps here, more than anywhere, Lily had subconsciously sought a way to remind herself that she was still married to another man—a man who, though she no longer believed it, might one day come back and claim her as his wife. Or had she done it as a secret admission that some part of her would always remain wedded to Saige and his memory?

Well, it hardly mattered anymore. Now she had something much more substantial to remind her— a flesh-and-blood husband. Did she still think Serendipity was the right name for Randall's mare?

"Saige?" Lily called, coming to her feet as she realized he and Crysta had left the corral and were riding up the trail.

"Back in a few minutes," he called, waving over his shoulder.

Lily started after them, then shrugged helplessly. Saige was helping Crysta, she reminded herself, when no one else could. And the sooner the little girl got back on a horse, the better.

Lily looked at her watch. The better for Crysta. She wasn't sure how it would work out for her and Randall.

An hour later, her patience gone, Lily walked to Saige's pickup and jerked open the door. *He* could go to the trouble of finding another way back to town—*she* was leaving now.

As she slid beneath the wheel, Invictus, hissing and spitting, rose stiffly to his feet. His back arched sharply and he let out a growling yowl. Unsheathing all his claws, he swiped at her bare arm.

Lily shrieked and leaped out of the truck. "You win, Invictus," she muttered through the window.

Invictus and now Crysta, Lily grumbled to herself. *If he keeps this up, he'll have a whole army of lost souls.*

By the time Lily heard horses coming around the barn, she could happily have strangled Saige. Randall was surely fuming by now, and Saige knew it. But he still hadn't returned. This was a group of dudes coming home from a day ride. Two of the ranch cowboys rode with them, and four of the summer kids.

"Shorty," Lily called to the lead rider. "Can I borrow a vehicle to get to town? My ride seems to have abandoned me."

Shorty cast an eye at the pickup. "That really Saige's?"

"Yes, and I'd have taken it by now if it didn't have such a threatening alarm system."

"Yes, ma'am," Shorty said, as if he didn't really understand. "Let me just get these horses taken care of."

Lily chewed her thumbnail waiting for the guests to dismount. It seemed to take forever for Shorty to get each horse in the charge of one of the kids. As the last horse was led away, Saige and Crysta appeared around the other side of the barn.

"Something wrong?" Saige asked innocently, looking from the impatient Lily to the nervous Shorty. He glanced at his watch. "Uh-oh, Crysta, I think I'm in trouble."

Too nettled to speak, Lily just glared at him.

Saige dismounted and lifted Crysta off. Handing her the reins, he said, "Do you think you can groom her tonight the way I told you without me helping you?"

Crysta nodded gravely, but she was obviously very anxious.

Saige regarded her a moment. "Maybe Shorty'd better groom her tonight." Shorty gave an affirmative nod in response to Saige's questioning look. "Tomorrow I'll ride my own horse and we'll groom them both together. Okay?"

"Fine, fine," Lily said impatiently. She stood with her hand on the door of the pickup tapping her toe. "C'mon, Saige."

"Okay, Crysta?" Saige asked. When the little girl nodded, Saige retrieved the reins from her tight grasp and led the mare over to Shorty. "See you tomorrow."

As he spoke, the familiar roar of Randall's Lamborghini reached Lily's ears. "Oh, no," she groaned, slumping against the side of the pickup. "Now you've made Randall drive all the way out here in that ridiculous car."

Saige's grin showed not a flicker of remorse. "Why doesn't he get something a little more sensible for the country roads?"

"Because he likes—" Lily ground her teeth. "It's none of your business what Randall likes to drive."

Saige held up his hands in mock surrender. "Hey, take it easy, Ms. Harmony. I was only asking. He can drive the Indy winner for all I care." He glanced at Crysta. "Since Lily's date has rescued her, how 'bout if I stay and help you groom your horse?"

Crysta's face lit up with smiles as Saige led Sera toward her.

Hoping to avoid any further confrontation, Lily walked to the passenger side of the Lamborghini as soon as it pulled into the stable yard. But Randall had other ideas.

"Just what the devil is going on here?" he demanded, unfolding himself from the sports car. He shot a look at Sera then back to Lily. "Were you riding, too?"

"No, dear," Lily said soothingly. "Crysta rode my horse."

"I've told these children they're not allowed to ride your horse, Lillabeth. They know that." He aimed a finger at his employee. "So do you, Shorty. How did this happen?"

"I took the girl for a ride on the gentlest horse I could see," Saige said from the door to the barn.

"I'll do it again tomorrow. I had permission from the horse's owner."

"The hell you did!" Randall snapped. "I don't want anyone else on that horse."

"Randall, I—" Lily began.

"The hell I didn't," Saige interrupted. "I understand the mare belongs to Lily. Or do you retract your gifts when things don't go your way?"

"Of course Sera belongs to Lillabeth," Randall said.

"They did ask me first, dear."

Randall swiveled his head, giving Lily the full blast of his irritation, irritation she strongly suspected had nothing to do with horses and a great deal to do with Saige.

"You know my wishes in the matter, Lillabeth."

"Serendipity," Saige mused, lips twitching as if he was holding back a grin. "I wonder if you know hers, Carver."

Randall narrowed his eyes at Saige's back as he and his two charges disappeared into the barn, followed rapidly by Shorty, who seemed eager to escape Randall's wrath.

When Randall again favored Lily with his look, his pique had not dimmed. "I think I deserve an explanation, Lillabeth."

"An explanation?" Lily slapped the car's roof, annoyed in the extreme by both these men. "For what? Being late for dinner? Not that I recall setting an exact time. But believe me, I'd've been there an hour ago if *I* had anything to say about it."

"An explanation," Randall said, enunciating each word carefully, though he did not raise his voice, "for what you were doing out here alone with your husband for hours."

"I wasn't alone with my husband," Lily said. "I was alone with the mountain lion he keeps to guard his truck. *He* was alone with Crysta and my horse. And as far as I'm concerned, Randall, she can ride the horse for the rest of her visit if it makes her feel better."

"I bought the horse for you because she was exceptionally gentle. I don't wish to have a lot of inexperienced children toughen her mouth or take her out when you want to ride her." Randall paused to take a deep, calming breath. "But that's beside the point, and you know it."

"No, I don't," Lily said, opening the passenger door to the sports car with a healthy tug. "I don't know what the point is at all. I've been sitting on that darn step for over an hour waiting for Saige to get back here with Crysta and take me home, and now you show up and treat me like a criminal. Maybe you should just take me home and we can forget dinner."

Randall eyed her a moment, then let his stiff shoulders slump. Coming around the car, he offered her a hand to help her into the seat, then shut the door for her without a slam.

When he'd belted himself behind the wheel, he took her hand and gave it a squeeze. "I understand why you're upset."

Lily tensed, almost pulling her fingers from Randall's grasp. Despite his sympathetic words, she sensed he was about to deliver a lecture she would rather not hear. But when she looked at their clasped hands and remembered that in a few weeks she meant to put her hand in his for life, she knew she was being unfair.

"I'm sorry I made you wait, Randall."

He smiled thinly. "You seem to spend an awful lot of time with this man you say you never want to see again." He held up a palm to stop her objections. "Last night you couldn't come to dinner with Dad because you had to take Pen out to Saige's ranch. You were so uncomfortable there, you hardly slept afterward, making you too tired again to have dinner with my father. Yet not so tired you couldn't drive all the way out here with Saige to sit on a step while I wait for you."

Randall's words stirred a jumble of thoughts in Lily's mind. She chewed her lip, feeling confused and contrite. "He said he wouldn't come unless I showed him the way," she said at last, knowing how weak that sounded.

"Lillabeth," he said reprovingly. "How hard did you try to dissuade him?"

Lily wanted to defend herself, but she couldn't help wondering if Randall was right. Was she lying to herself? To Randall? Had she come to the dude ranch because Saige insisted or simply because she wanted to spend time with him?

"I shouldn't have come," she agreed. "I knew that as soon as I saw them ride off up the trail. But it was too late by then." She put her hand behind Randall's neck and pulled his head toward her. When he resisted, she gave him a peck on the cheek. "We can go to your parents' for dinner. I never meant any rudeness to your father."

Randall looked at his watch. "It's a little late for that, dear. Perhaps we'll drop by after we eat our cold stir-fried shrimp." He gave her a look of mild accusation.

"Of course," she forced herself to say, "I'd love to pay your parents a visit."

Truly Lily enjoyed Ran, Randall's father, and had never felt uncomfortable in his company as she often did with Kokie. But tonight she'd far rather have skipped any visiting, even with Randall, and gone home to her own apartment where no one would require polite conversation from her or explanations of her behavior or even coherent thought. For that matter, she didn't even feel much like eating.

Surely this agony couldn't last forever. She would get used to seeing Saige alive and not feel her heart leap to her throat every time he appeared. He'd realize she meant it when she said they were through and he'd stop seeking her out. And sooner or later, Saige would regain his hunger for adventure and leave Deep Water for good.

Lily longed for the day. She was sure she did.

An hour later, after pushing food around on her plate, Lily put it down on the smoked glass coffee table and leaned back into the corner of Randall's soft leather couch, plumping the cushions around her. "I may never move again." She sighed.

Randall flicked up a brow. "If you wish to spend the night, sweetheart, you don't need to ask with such subtlety."

Lily chuckled, then turned serious. "I've always been very grateful, Randall, that you didn't push me... that way."

"It hasn't been easy." His voice deepened as he moved up the couch beside her, his thigh against hers pressing her farther into the corner. "But I knew how brittle you were in that regard. Besides, it is the sort of trait one's glad to find in one's future wife—forsaking all others and all that."

"It'd seem even more of an infidelity now," Lily said. "With my husband alive and—"

"You don't need to remind me, Lillabeth," Randall interrupted.

Cupping her chin, he pressed kisses from her temple to her ear. His breath felt hot then cold against the inner whorls, making her shiver against him.

With a sound of male satisfaction, Randall tipped her head into the cushions, and his mouth descended. His lips encircled hers, covering them with wetness and heat, while his tongue stiffened to dart in and out of her mouth. Groans came from him.

As he deepened the kiss, crushing her lips against her teeth, Lily raised her hands to his shoulders, trying to hold him away. The gentleness Randall usually exercised with her seemed for once entirely absent. His kiss felt hard and urgent, and it hurt. Despite the pressure of her hands, Randall settled his weight on her heavily as he covered her body with his and thrust his hips forward with rough, lunging motions.

He seemed lost in his own world, wholly unaware of Lily, who felt as if she couldn't breathe. More shocked than truly frightened, but struggling to bring Randall to his senses, she tried to writhe out from under him. His fierce embrace trapped her beneath him. Moaning loudly, Randall ground his arousal against her pubic bone.

"Randall," she cried, "you're hurting me."

He froze. "Oh, God," he murmured, rolling off her at once. "I'm sorry, Lillabeth. I don't know what came over me."

"You've never acted like that before." Still shaken, Lily let him press her cheek to his chest.

Randall held her a moment, cursing very softly under his breath. "I didn't mean to frighten you. I just..."

Lily pulled back to see his face. He looked away from her, as if ashamed to meet her eyes. "What, Randall? Tell me. I hardly think you're an animal because you got a little carried away with me one time." She reached to pat his cheek. "I'd feel a lot worse if you *didn't* want me."

Randall stood and walked toward the windows. Without turning around, he jammed both hands in his pockets, tightening the shirt across his shoulders. "I want you, Lillabeth. I have from the moment I saw you at the ranch the day I came out to meet Warren."

"You couldn't have wanted me *that* day," Lily protested. "I was such a mess."

"You did look more bedraggled than I'd ever seen a beautiful woman allow herself to look. Your hair was stringy and unwashed, you'd let yourself go to skin and bone, you wore those awful baggy clothes of your husband's." He came toward her. "Even so, I wanted to rip the clothes off you and take you right there on the floor."

"Randall, you never told me that before," Lily said. "I'm sure no one in Deep Water has any idea those kinds of thoughts lurk behind your proper exterior."

"Even you, Lillabeth? I love you." He gripped her head between his hands. "Why does it surprise you that I want you?"

Lily shook her head. "I just didn't know...it was that strong in you."

"I want you...*need* you tonight, Lillabeth. I've waited long enough." He dropped his hands to her shoulders and lifted her off the couch. Her feet barely touched the floor as he held her to him. "Let's go upstairs. I won't be rough this time."

"Need?" A wave of panic washed over Lily. "Why need, Randall? Why now?"

"I need to know you still love me." He lowered her till she stood. "If *he* hadn't come back, I'd wait until we married. But now...with him here and you so entangled in your former relationship... I need to have you make this commitment to me."

Randall slipped an arm around her waist and led her toward the stairs. Lily let herself be pulled along, dreading what was to come. If she had been swept away by emotion and passion and made love to Randall on the couch, she wouldn't mind. She would even be glad of it because it would make Randall believe she loved him.

But this seemed so cold and unfeeling—simply a way for Randall to prove his virility to Saige. It had nothing to do with Lily, and it made her feel used.

She put her hand on the banister and stopped them before the first step. "When will I be divorced?"

"I meant to speak to you about that," Randall said. He turned her in his arms. "I'll explain later."

"No, now," Lily insisted. "So I'll understand why you can't wait."

"Montana law only permits the quick divorce when there's no property or children. The Alexander ranch complicates the process. It's half yours, you know."

"Yes, I know, but of course I won't— I don't want..." Lily choked on the words, knowing she'd never feel at home there again, understanding as Randall never would how many dreams would die with one signature. "I'll sign it over to him."

"It doesn't matter. We have to go through a more complicated proceeding." Randall was sounding more lawyerly and less passionate by the minute. He sat on the stairs and pulled her down beside him. "It doesn't have to take much longer. A few weeks more should do it. But only if Saige goes along. If he causes any problem, the thing could take months."

"I see." A rush of cold hit Lily, and she withdrew her hand from Randall's, feeling suddenly like a bone between two scrapping dogs. "You want me tonight because you think Saige won't fight the divorce if he finds out we're sleeping together."

"I want you, Lillabeth, because I love you beyond words." Randall stood, pulling her with him. "I don't know how long we'll have to wait to get married and I can't wait any longer to indulge the physical side of our relationship." He tugged her up the bottom step.

Lily looked up the staircase that wrapped around two sides of the living room. Randall's bedroom was at the top of the stairs, taking up a full half of the second floor. The room was beautiful, with its skylight over the bed and the glass doors facing the mountains. She'd been there dozens of times for innocuous reasons.

Did she want to go there now? Whether her divorce took a few weeks or a few months, she'd go to this room with Randall in a very short time and do just what he was proposing they do tonight. She'd already agreed to divorce Saige. All they needed now was a final decree. What earthly difference would a piece of paper make?

After all, she could see she'd made Randall wait far too long already. Hadn't he just nearly lost control on the couch? That was surely Lily's fault, she understood that.

In her deepest thoughts, Lily acknowledged she had waited all these years, made Randall wait, hoping, praying for Saige's return. But he *had* returned, he was here now. And nothing had changed. Lily could not forgive him his desertion, or risk the emotional torment loving him again would bring.

Randall was right. In a few weeks, *he* would be her husband, not Saige. What better way to prove to both these men—and even more, to herself—that she was over Saige, their past together forgotten, than to allow Randall to make love to her tonight?

Her future husband gave another tug on her arm, and Lily followed him up the stairs.

CHAPTER SEVEN

AT THE side of his bed, Randall pulled Lily into his arms for a kiss. She'd kissed him many times before. Why did tonight seem so different?

For the first time, Lily was sorry Saige had ever come home. Of course she'd always known, without acknowledging it, that Randall's kisses did not move her as Saige's had. But when Randall first kissed her, she hadn't wished for such passion. Rather she'd needed the tenderness and concern he'd always shown her.

And she'd confidently expected that after they were married, when their familiarity with each other increased, the passion would come. Didn't all married couples grow more aware of each other's needs over the years? Hadn't she and Saige needed time to grow comfortable with the physical side of love?

Lily squeezed her eyes shut and hugged Randall closer, for she knew that wasn't true. She remembered far too well the sweep of passions that flooded her the first time Saige kissed her. It wasn't an easy kiss to forget.

He'd come home from college to take her to the prom her junior year in high school. She'd never have dared to ask him. But when he came home for spring break and learned she'd never gone to a prom, he said she was too beautiful to sit home. All the boys in her class must be idiots, he declared. Speechless with delight, Lily didn't dare tell him how many dates she'd turned down, waiting for him.

The night had been magic. A typical Montana prom night, it snowed four inches and the mercury dropped nearly to zero. She'd worn a lavender dress that made her look like a princess, covered with a red down jacket. Saige wore a black tuxedo with a cummerbund that matched her dress, and heavy Sorrel boots. Their parents laughed at their half-formal attire, and so did they.

The kiss hadn't happened till the fifth slow song they danced together. Lily had counted. She could remember each dance. Every minute she spent in his arms made her more sure of her love for him. Each dance, Saige pulled her closer, each dance, she relaxed more against him.

The fifth dance, he linked his hands behind her, resting them warm and heavy in the small of her back. She laced hers together around his neck. With her head on his shoulder, she suddenly heard herself whispering into his ear all the love she'd felt for him for so long.

Obviously startled, Saige took her head between his palms and held her where he could see her eyes. "You don't mean that."

"I mean it, Saige Alexander. I've loved you since kindergarten." Her cheeks flamed beneath his fingers. "Don't you remember the day you got my doll back from those bullies?"

"No." He smiled weakly. "Well, maybe, kind of."

She could tell he didn't remember at all. But she didn't care. "Well, I remember. And I know you think I'm crazy but that's how I feel. So if you want to take me home now, you can." She eyed the red stripe across the gym floor.

"Take you home?" Saige sounded incredulous. "I'd like to take you to the fishing access, but it's too cold."

Lily looked up, afraid to hope. "The fishing access?"

"Haven't you ever been to the river with a boy, you innocent?"

"I've never gone anywhere with a boy, Saige," she said, fighting the urge to return her gaze to her feet. "I've never liked any other boy but you." Slowly she licked her lips as she had seen other girls do with their boyfriends. When Saige's hungry gaze locked on the movements of her tongue, she began to understand why. She lowered her voice. "What would we do at the fishing access, Saige?"

He laughed, but it wasn't his usual easygoing laugh. As naive as she was, Lily heard the difference. It was deeper and huskier and rich with sexual overtone.

"It's time someone showed you," he said. "I'm glad I get to be the one."

Without taking his hands from her face, he kissed her where they stood. It started sweetly enough, just a brushing of the lips. The kind of kiss Lily had dreamed about since fifth grade. But the sweetness turned to passion with lightning speed. His arms moved around her waist to pull her tight, and her hands trembled against his stiff formal shirt.

When Lily opened her lips to Saige's urging and let him press his kiss inside her, she wasn't shocked. Overwhelmed, swamped, deluged, but not shocked. Nothing had ever felt so right.

Who knows how long they'd have stood with their mouths joined if the music hadn't ended. Not that they noticed. What they noticed was the sound of all their friends clapping at this unabashed demonstration of love. Lily clung to Saige still, but he very tenderly pulled away from her.

"Maybe we'd better not go to the river," he murmured.

Lily barely heard him over the pounding of her heart, but one of the chaperones had no trouble. "I should say not, young man. You'll keep Lily right here. Or shall I call her father to come pick her up?"

Lily remembered the intrusive voice of Old Miss Elephant Ears with a jolt.

Randall lifted his head to gaze at her questioningly. "What is it, sweet?"

"I can't do this, Randall. I don't understand it myself. I just feel ... married, whether I want it or not. I gave my word." She looked at him, begging for understanding. "We've waited years. What's a few more weeks?" She plopped down on the edge of the king-size bed. "I feel like the prize in a contest between you and my ex-husband."

Randall looked stricken. "Do you think that's the only reason I want you?"

Lily smiled at him. "I hope not." She braced her hands beside her on the bed. "Randall, if you tell me honestly that this has nothing to do with proving something to Saige, that you want me tonight, not on our wedding night as we've planned for so long, just because you love me, then I'll ..." She shrugged. "I'll go buy you the condom myself."

"Buy one?" Randall snatched open his bedside table drawer. "What do you think those are, after-dinner mints? Do you think I wouldn't protect you?"

Lily had only a quick glance at the scatter of small foil packets before Randall shut the drawer.

"I didn't think about it before," she said, embarrassed. "I... Thank you, Randall."

"Don't thank me, since I don't get to use one."
He let out a long breath. "You're right. I do want to prove to Saige that you're mine. And to you."
He shook his head. "I know how important it is to you for our wedding night to be perfect. I don't want to ruin that for you." He offered her a hand and pulled her to her feet. "But you'd better get off my bed, Lillabeth, before I forget all about restraint."

Lily sat on the back steps at her apartment, musing disconsolately. Her apartment took up the rear half of a beautiful old house, the first brick house ever built in Deep Water, surrounded by huge aged pines and willows. Through the branches, she could just see the alluvial fan that formed the peak of Baldy Mountain.

Today was Wednesday. She should be riding the trails below that fan. But she couldn't.

Nor could she take her quarter horse, Sera, somewhere else to ride, because she'd promised Crysta she could ride the horse as long as she stayed at the dude ranch. Besides, where else could she take her horse?

Lily swivelled her gaze to the west. Though she couldn't see anything in this direction besides pine branches, she knew that sixteen miles away, as the crow flew, Saige's ranch was situated. Her ranch, too, for a few more weeks—till Saige agreed to a divorce and she gave up all her rights to it.

But, even if she hadn't promised Crysta, Saige's ranch was the *last* place she should go riding. If he saw her and joined her, especially on horseback, the memories would swamp her.

Lily stared at her soft old cowboy boots and thought about changing into her aerobic shoes. She had to do something besides sit on the back steps feeling sorry for herself. Riding was her favorite exercise, and she usually got to do it three days a week, except in the dead of winter. She loved the smell of the horses and the sounds of the saddle and the clomp of hooves along the trail.

She shook her head. Surely she could find a substitute for a few weeks.

A second pair of cowboy boots, older and more worn, joined hers on the walk. Lily didn't need to look up to know Saige stood above her. Neither she nor Grace had ever had the fortitude to throw away those boots. They'd been sitting in the mudroom, getting dryer and duller, for seven years.

Saige spoke to the top of her head. "Did you see our old horse trailer go by the other day?"

"Uh-huh," Lily said to the boots. "Where did you get it? I thought Warren sold everything."

"Nope," Saige said. "Lots of old stuff in the barn. Like that tractor you saw me on. Remember—"

"I remember, Saige." Lily cut him off. She didn't want to remember anything connected with the old tractor, whether from seven days or seven years ago.

"'Course, what he *did* sell," Saige went on as though she hadn't uttered a word, "were the cows and the horses and the dogs and Mom's goat. Since he was leaving for most of the year and you didn't want to—"

"I know he sold the animals." Growing irritated, Lily looked up at last. "Did you want something, Saige? Is that why you dropped by?"

"Did I want something?" A grin curled one side of his lips as he pushed his Stetson to the back of his head with a forefinger. "You mean I haven't made myself clear? Damn right I want something. I want—"

"Saige!" Lily stood and climbed the three steps to her door, determined to avoid this turn to the conversation.

"Hey, Blue," Saige said. "Your uncertainty is showing. If you're so sure of your choice, why do you keep running away from me?"

"I'm not running away." Without taking her hand from the door latch, she turned to face him. "I simply promised my fiancé, quite reasonably I think, that I wouldn't have any more private meetings with you."

"Private?" Saige looked up and down the street. "In full view of all your neighbors? This is Deep Water, Blue. Nothing that's happened here in the last hundred and twenty years has stayed private." He put one foot on the step and leaned his forearms on his knee. "Before that it was private only because no one lived here."

"You know what I mean." Lily released the latch and leaned against the door. "Without him around."

"Well, I think it's damn silly," Saige said. "If your relationship is that tenuous, you ought to call off the wedding. But I figured something like that had happened when you quit coming to the dude ranch. Shorty told me you used to ride all the time."

Lily glanced at her boots. "I did, but..." She let the sentence hang.

"Don't you miss it, Blue?"

She hooked her thumbs into her denim pockets. "Yes, but I promised Crysta my horse. And Kokie—"

"Kokie?" Saige interrupted, his anger not disguised by the softness of his voice. "What the hell did she have to do with this decision? Is that who you're engaged to—Kokie?"

"Of course not. She just said... She and Ran both... We stopped by to see them the other night, after I took you to the dude ranch."

Thoughts of that visit set Lily's teeth on edge. They'd gone straight to Kokie's from Randall's bedroom, and she'd still felt his tension—and hers—over her refusal to make love with him. Ran had been charming, as always, but Lily had sensed a real edge to Kokie's welcome, especially after she learned Lily had spent the afternoon with Saige at the dude ranch.

But though it *was* Kokie who suggested that Lily stay away from the horse camp while Saige worked there, Lily would never have gone along if Randall hadn't agreed with his mother. Lily promised Randall because she loved him, she reminded herself. Even Ran, who never interfered, thought the decision a wise one.

"Ran's only here a few weeks every summer," she said, musing out loud.

Saige raised his brows. "Does that remark tie up somehow?"

"Tie up?" Jolted to the present, Lily put her hands on her hips. "I don't owe you an explanation of my actions, Saige Alexander. If I don't want to ride for the summer, that's my business."

Saige held up both his hands. "I won't argue that," he agreed. "But I'm glad you've got some strength of character left. At least it took all three of them ganging up on you to get you to decide something so stupid."

Lily raised her chin. "You only think it's stupid because you don't understand. Or won't."

He ran his gaze up and down her stiff form at the top of the steps and held a hand out to her. "Come back here and sit down, will you? You look like a bird about to fly away. I'm not Invictus, for God's sake. I'm not going to pounce on you."

Refusing his hand, Lily returned to the bottom step and sat down.

"Don't you feel a little like a caged pet of the Carver family?" Saige asked, his tone as casual as if he was asking about the weather.

"No!" She'd have risen again except Saige put a hand on her shoulder and held her down. "Kokie didn't gang up on me, not really. She just noticed that when I'm around you, I get all...rattled. It upsets me to see you, Saige."

"I'm damn glad to hear it, love," he said, a smile softening his features. "You have no idea what seeing you does to me."

Lily covered her face with both hands. "I don't want to feel this way," she mumbled. "It hurts, Saige, I don't like it. Kokie said she could tell when I walked through the door that I wasn't as...tranquil. And she knew at once I'd seen you that day."

Instead of leaving quietly as she'd expected him to do... Well, no, when Lily really thought about it, she didn't expect Saige to back off easily. When had he ever? He didn't now, either.

Gripping her wrists, he pulled her hands down and held them in her lap. "If they're all so scared of you seeing me, doesn't that make you understand there's still too much between us to give up? God almighty, if Kokie realizes it, what will it take to make *you* realize it?" She tugged at her wrists, but he wouldn't let go. "Look at you, you're trembling all over."

"That's because I'm going back on my promise to Randall!"

"No, it's not, Lily, and you know it." Saige released her wrists. "It's because I can't put my hands on you without making you want me bad enough to tremble." He held his shaking hand out. "It happens to me, too."

Lily would have gone inside then, but she wasn't sure her legs would get her up the stairs. "I'd never suggest I'm unaffected by you, Saige. I did love you once. So much that I was always afraid. I don't want to do that to Randall, to make him worry all the time."

"You worried I'd leave the country and *take you with me,*" Saige said. "You never worried about me being with other women. You didn't have to."

"Randall always puts my feelings first," Lily insisted. "I can do the same for him this once."

"That pompous self-centered ass?" Saige's tone echoed with cynicism. "When does he put your feelings first?"

"Why, just that night," Lily exclaimed, determined to defend her love and her decisions, "just an hour before, when I asked him not to—"

She clamped her lips shut, feeling heat rush up her neck and throb in her cheeks. Dear Lord, how could she let Saige distract her so? She'd almost revealed intimate details of her relationship with Randall. To *Saige*. She shuddered when she thought of the turn his teasing would take then.

One eyebrow was raised nearly to his hairline. Saige gave her an odd look, filled with intense curiosity, but tinged with confidence, as well. Could he read her thoughts? He certainly found humor in her remark. He was smiling broadly.

"When you asked him not to what, Blue? You might as well tell me, I have a damn good idea anyway." He stroked the side of his finger down her flaming cheek. "You look just like you did when Mom caught us in the barn."

Lily glared at him, trying to replace whatever expression he thought he could see on her face with one of rage. She couldn't say a word.

"I'm glad to hear *you* asked him not to, love. I'd have asked him myself if I thought it would do any good." Saige's voice sounded thick with laughter he tried for a moment to control. Then he threw back his head and let it out, loud and happy and utterly satisfied.

"I don't know why you keep coming around here bothering me, Saige Alexander," Lily said furiously, when he finally brought his mirth under control. "We can't even have a conversation without you insulting Randall and his family. *My* family soon. No wonder he doesn't want me to see you." She stood. "I love him too much to hurt him the way *you* always hurt me. And if you think I'm going to just let you waltz back into my life and hurt me that much again, you're crazy!"

Saige's grin faded, and his shoulders slumped. "I never want to hurt you, Blue."

"If you'll excuse me," Lily went on, ignoring her guilt at the fresh pain she heard in his voice, "I was just going to put on my running shoes."

"Don't go," Saige said, all the tease gone from his voice. "I won't say another word about Carver or his family."

"Promise?"

He held up three fingers of his right hand. "Scout's honor." He gestured at her feet. "And don't bother with your running shoes. You can still ride."

"But I promised Crysta."

"It doesn't matter. I take my horse out to the dude ranch now, that's why I need the horse trailer. You can have—"

Lily frowned as the import of Saige's words hit her. "What horse?"

"Virago." Years seemed to melt away from Saige's face. "I found him and bought him back." He lifted his right shoulder in a shrug. "His owner'd never been able to ride him anyway, said he was a devil."

"He *was* a devil," Lily agreed. "None of us could ever ride him, either, after you left."

"Not even Dad?"

"I don't think he ever tried," Lily said. "It made him too sad."

The soft look in Saige's eyes disappeared. He dropped the subject. "Virago was sad, too, when

I put him in the trailer all alone. I could tell how lonely he was back there."

"Aren't you exaggerating a bit, Saige?"

"I'm pretty sensitive to that emotion these days," he insisted. "So I also bought the horse he'd shared a corral with the last four years." He gave her a quick grin. "I want him to be happy."

"You bought a horse for your horse?" Lily shook a finger at him. "Don't get that attached to your calves next year, or you won't show much profit."

"I wanted her anyway, Blue."

He took Lily's hand then, making her acknowledge inwardly that no matter what subject Saige talked about, this meeting was still way too private to satisfy her promise to Randall. So private, she should pull her hand away and go inside.

Instead she took Saige's bait. "Why did you want the other horse?"

He gave her a smile so poignant it hurt. "It was Serendipity. I couldn't separate them."

"Serendipity?" Lily's voice came out half-gasp, half-sigh. "Don't." She jerked her hand free.

Lily bit her lip, fighting memories. She hadn't wanted Warren to sell her horse with the other ranch animals, but Randall had convinced her cutting all attachment to the ranch would make her happier in the long run. That's when he had promised to buy her another horse.

"I ride Virago at the dude ranch every day, Lily. I won't ride at home. I'll stay away any evenings you want to ride. You can have the ranch to yourself. I won't bother you."

"It's not your ranch," Lily protested. "Not legally. It's leased."

"I've talked to the lessors. They don't care if we ride. Alone or together." He put his hands on her upper arms, squeezing softly. Warmth slid down her arms, over her back. "I couldn't take Virago and leave her there, Blue, all by herself. They've always shared a corral. And she's... we...I had to bring her." He put the edge of his hand beneath her chin, urging her to look at him. "She's yours, Blue. Whenever you want to ride her, whenever you want to take her away. That's all I came to say."

With that, he removed the unwanted touch of his hands on her face and shoulders and walked toward his pickup. Lily put her own hand where his had touched her chin, angry at the goose bumps that shivered down her arms at his withdrawal. She gazed at his form, noticing against her will that the denim across his thighs and hips looked tauter than it had a few days ago.

When he climbed into the cab of his truck, Invictus yowled a welcome. Saige slammed the door. "Your saddle's in the barn," he called out the window.

As he drove slowly down the road, Invictus climbed onto his shoulders and curled around his neck. Lily ran inside before she could let herself wish *she* were the one curling around Saige's body.

CHAPTER EIGHT

SAIGE stopped his pickup in the circular drive and glared. So this was Kokie's place. Beautiful logs, beautiful landscaping. And as out of place as he'd expected. The damn porch, despite its phony hitching rails, looked like an antebellum veranda, and the flowers in the beds in front looked like they'd been chosen to match the floral upholstery on the porch furniture. None of which looked a damn bit appropriate with hand-peeled spruce logs.

Swearing liberally, Saige cut off his thoughts. He'd find fault with Kokie's residence no matter how attractive. Just as he found fault with her son, though he'd heard nothing but good about the man. Not effusive, but good. Honest, hardworking, word as good as gold, reliable as hell.

All the things Lily'd look for in a husband . . . a second husband, anyway. Because what she really hungered for was half a world away, letting her down, hour by hour, day by day, till she learned never to trust those wants again.

Saige slammed the door on those thoughts, too. When he'd gotten Kokie's handwritten note inviting him to this little tête à tête, he'd felt a violent desire not to go. Especially after Lily's description of *her* last conversation with Kokie. But Kokie had made it sound as if Lily's happiness was at stake, and Saige couldn't take the risk she might be right.

But he knew, as soon as he saw the return address engraved on the heavy cream stationery, that he had to turn off all emotions, hide any memories that struggled to surface, or he wouldn't get through the meeting.

He scratched Invictus behind the ears. "I promise," he said. "I'll keep the lid on. Just don't eat anyone's flesh while I'm gone. Got it, buddy?"

Invictus made the growling noise that seemed to pass for a purr with him. Saige lowered the windows partway for him and left the truck. Mounting the steps, he let a wall come down in his mind between the moment at hand and everything in his life that mattered. No matter what she said, he would not let Kokie touch him where it hurt.

His first thought when she opened the door to his knock, shooing away the maid, was, Crysta hadn't been kidding, the woman's hair really was pink. Repressing his surprise got him through introductions and into the living room.

Despite his desire not to accept her hospitality, he numbly took a glass of iced tea because it was easier than arguing and easier to think about than where he was and who he was with. He could tell from his grip on the tumbler it was made of crystal. Expensive as hell, he guessed. She probably paid a lot for imported tea, too, though he could hardly taste it.

Saige noticed Kokie's lips moving and quit thinking about tea. He couldn't care less what she drank, and the sooner he paid attention to what she was saying, the sooner he could get out of here.

"...upset her a great deal. More than you know I'm sure, Mr. Alexander."

He put his glass down on a porcelain coaster, glad he didn't, in his anger, smash the delicate piece. He wouldn't let his rage out in his voice, either. "You're wrong. I understand very well how upset she is and what she's going through now, because I know what she gave up when I left. *You* have no idea. I understand her pain more intensely than anyone, because I know her better than anyone." Without blinking, he stared into Kokie's pale hazel eyes. "Better than your son, God knows."

Kokie's lips drew together into a wrinkled little circle. She, too, must be trying to control emotions. "She no longer loves you, Mr. Alexander. She wishes to marry Randall, and no one who knows the two of you would dispute her choice."

Saige shook his head. "Wrong again, lady. Want me to circulate a petition?"

"You seem to find this all very amusing." Kokie drew herself up stiffly, tightening the Hawaiian print blouse over her ample bosom. "I personally do not find the distress Lily is suffering at the moment a bit funny."

Saige let his back teeth take all his rage. "I don't find it funny, either. What do you suggest? Shall I kill myself to get out of the way? Or have you already hired a hit man?"

"I suggest you leave the valley." Kokie put her glass down so hard tea spilled onto the table.

"My ranch is here," Saige said. "I own it free and clear. A home, a job. Why would I leave?"

"You owe it to Lily," Kokie pronounced. "I am prepared to buy you out. How many acres do you own? Just over three thousand, I believe. Plus some forest allotments? I'll give you a million and a half for it. All of it. That's more than it's worth, and you know it."

Wrath filled Saige with such fierceness his stomach lurched. He kept his lips and teeth tight together till the wave of nausea passed. "This must be a scene from a movie, right? You want to buy my wife from me for a few million bucks? It's got to be a comedy. Maybe a documentary on white slavery." He stood. "Thanks for the tea."

"Mr. Alexander, wait!"

Saige kept walking. Her contrition caught him at the archway.

"I'm sorry, Mr. Alexander. That was unforgivable. But please. Think of Lily!"

He didn't want to respond. He should keep moving. But he couldn't. "I *am* thinking of her, God damn it." He didn't turn around. "I think of nothing else."

Kokie's breath left her body audibly. "I know that." He heard her rise. "But you're not thinking clearly." She was right behind him. His skin crawled with her closeness. "Let us assume for a moment that Lily means it when she says she wants to marry Randall. Will you make that assumption for the sake of discussion?"

Saige forced emotion from his face. "Yes." He turned.

She looked tense, her pink-tipped nails folded into her palms, then back out. "Every time Lily sees you, she grows more unhappy. But she does not weaken in her resolve. You are destroying her tranquillity, not changing her mind."

Saige regarded Kokie coldly, silently.

"If you love her, and I believe you do, let her go, Mr. Alexander. It's what she wants." The nails squeezed into fists again. "Let her make her choice unhampered. Don't fight the divorce. Don't rub more guilt in her wounds by playing upon her sympathies. That's all she feels for you now, but she feels it most intensely."

"Anything else?" Saige asked, his voice thick with sarcasm. "The rest of the land in the valley? Death of all the firstborn?"

"Make jokes if you wish, but you know I'm right. And whatever you decide..." She looked suddenly very ill-at-ease. "I'd appreciate it if you didn't tell her of this visit. Or... my son."

"Randall doesn't even know?" Saige asked, grinning at last. "That raises him some in my estimation."

He let the screen door slam behind him, walking quickly to get to his pickup before she said anything else, maybe something that would launch his anger to the surface. He didn't make it.

Kokie chased him out onto the porch. "If you decide after they're married that you do not wish to remain in Deep Water, my offer will still stand." She wrapped her hands around the railing. "I might even go higher. Say two million."

Saige spun the pickup around, throwing gravel into her perfect flower beds, and pushed the accelerator to the floor.

Lily stared down at the document in her lap, too numb for tears. Somehow this stunned her more than the idea of having Saige declared dead. Perhaps because she'd spent so many years readying herself for that procedure.

This came as a total shock.

"You did say," Randall asked, "that you would willingly give up your interest in the ranch, didn't you, Lillabeth?"

"Yes, of course."

"After all, he's agreed to let you divorce him without contest," Randall went on. "You certainly don't need that ranch, when I have three that will one day be half yours."

"It's not the real estate," Lily said. "It's just such a surprise. What made him change his mind?"

"I have no idea, my dear."

"He didn't say anything?"

Randall shook his head. "He was . . . terse on the phone. Simply said he wouldn't fight the divorce. Not that I cared to pursue it." He shrugged. "I suppose the reality of the situation came home to him at last."

"Reality?" Lily asked, wondering why she could not seem to absorb this conversation.

Randall cleared his throat. "My guess is that he's already growing bored with Deep Water and realizes he could never stay here for the long term, even to make you happy."

Tears blurred the letters on the property settlement, but Lily did not shed them. Whatever for? Hadn't she known Saige would tire of Deep Water sooner or later? It might be a little sooner than she'd expected, but she'd never really believed he meant to stay.

"Is there a problem, sweetheart?" Randall asked. "I thought we resolved all this. Does it upset you to think of the ranch in other hands?

If Saige doesn't wish to remain in Deep Water, shall I ask him if he'd let you keep the ranch?"

"It's not mine to keep, Randall. It was only mine while I was married to Saige. I'd never try to take it from him. Or Warren and Grace." She pulled in a long, calming breath and let it out slowly. "No, I just need a day or so to adjust to this. Today's Saturday, you can't file anything today anyway. I'll sign all this stuff on Monday."

Randall regarded her oddly. Then he rose, just as if she was a business appointment. She could tell he was angry but trying not to show it. He came around the desk and held out a hand to help her to her feet. Very courtly. She wondered how many times he'd used the gesture with clients.

"Very well." Randall gave her fingers a squeeze. "Shall I see you for dinner?"

"Of course. My apartment." She gave him a bright smile. "You have to get used to my cooking sometime."

He smiled back, just as brightly. "Of course."

As she turned off the highway, Lily shuddered, remembering the meeting. *Meeting!* she thought in dismay. When had she begun thinking of the time she spent with Randall as meetings?

Probably it had seemed like a business meeting because they'd had the discussion in his office about business matters. Is that the way she'd feel after they were married? At home they'd have a relationship and in his office they'd have meetings?

Lily tried to remember business discussions with Saige. They must have had them. All husbands and wives did, didn't they?

She certainly remembered the talks they'd had about Saige's desire to find a job overseas and her wish to stay right where she was. Those discussions had not been nearly as calm or as civilized as the one she'd had today with Randall. Yet even with tears and shouting and once...

Even alone in the car, Lily blushed thinking about *that* one. She and Saige had been arguing furiously in a half-mowed hay field far from the ranch house. She'd gotten so angry, she actually kicked him in the shin—not *really* hard, but maybe a little harder than she'd intended. Then she spun around to walk away, a tactical blunder. Saige retaliated instantly by applying a stinging swat to her bottom.

The next seconds, Lily couldn't remember very well. But at the end of about a minute, they were rolling in the sweet-smelling grass, kissing till she thought she'd die if he wouldn't make love to her right there. But he would.

Still, with all that yelling and kissing and rolling, they'd found a compromise. He would find a job and a place for them to live overseas, then she'd join him. She didn't really mind living out of the country for a few years, she just couldn't handle not having a nest. She'd come when he'd found them a nest. He left Montana, swearing their weeks apart would be the longest of his life. How prophetic that had turned out!

Lily stopped the car at the edge of the gravel road and watched Saige piloting the old tractor. What was he doing now?

Watching the chisel-shaped plow carve the dirt into small black hills, she had to wonder if she and Saige were destined to conduct all their important conversations in a hay field. Of course, this field was doubtless a safer place than his living room, or hers. Or downtown at the Buffalo Café, where half the town would hear in her voice that her heart was breaking because Saige wanted to divorce her.

Lily chewed her thumbnail, acknowledging what she couldn't in Randall's office—that learning Saige had agreed to divorce her had torn her up inside, and wondering why that was true. She'd told Saige, and Randall and Dana, and even Kokie, for that matter, that this was just what she wanted. Why did it hurt so much to get it?

Saige swung the tractor around at the end of a row and saw her car. He waved but kept plowing, turning his back to her to watch the blade cut through the earth behind him. Lily climbed through the fence and approached him slowly, not sure exactly what she wanted to say.

When she came close, Saige turned off the tractor and climbed down. "Damn quack grass," he grumbled, kicking at a tire. "Cut it, turn it up, cut it again—it still comes back."

"That's what you're doing now?" she asked, avoiding the real subject. "Killing quack grass?"

"I wish I was," he said irritably. "Just slowing it down. This is the fourth time I've turned the roots up to die in the sun, and it'll still come back in a few years. Always does. No way to get it all." He let out a long, frustrated breath and regarded her. "You came out here for a lesson in weeds, did you?"

Lily shook her head. "No. I..." She looked at him. "Randall told me."

"And?" Saige raised a brow, offering no comfort, no assistance. "You got what you wanted. Why come out here and pester me?"

"I didn't sign the papers."

"You didn't?" Saige put his hands on his hips. "What do you want now, half the ranch?"

"No," Lily said. "I want to know what changed your mind."

"You're something, you know that?" Saige gave a mirthless laugh. "What did you want me to do? Keep fighting the divorce so you could beat me in court? Do you need it public to prove something to yourself?"

"Saige," Lily begged. "Don't talk like that. You know that's not true."

His hands curled into fists. "I can't force you to love me, Blue."

Lily stared at Saige's rigid stance, at the muscle twitching in his uncovered chest. "This hurts you, too," she said almost to herself.

"Damn it, woman!" Saige roared. "Of course it hurts me, too."

At the sudden anguish in his voice, Lily stepped back, banging into the tractor. The clang made Saige flinch, but he recovered in an instant. Coldness shuttered any expression in his eyes. She knew it would be useless to ask again what distressed him about that noise.

"I expected you to get tired of ranching," she said. "Like what you said just now about the quack grass, about how useless it all is."

"I did *not* say it was useless." Saige bit the words out. "I simply pointed out it would have to be done again. I did not for a second imply that I was unwilling to do it."

Lily ignored his interruption, needing to make him understand what frightened her about him. "Hearing all that frustration in you, all that restlessness... It just confirms my fears. That's the kind of thing you used to say all the time." She ran her fingertip around a small rusted circle in the yellow paint of the tractor. "You're already getting bored."

"I am *not* bored." Frustration sharpened his tone, but she could tell the frustration was with her, not his task. "You'll never understand how much I love ranching. Working outside, watching life renew itself, taking part in something so elemental as growing food for people to eat." He was shouting again, shaking a fist. "I love it!"

Lily swallowed, awed by his vehemence. She could see the pulse pounding at the hollow in his neck. She desperately wanted to believe him. But she'd heard this sort of passion from him before—just before he left for South America.

"Listen to you." She sighed. "You sound so...aggravated, as if you were working up quite a snit before I got here."

"Snit?" Saige said. "Snit my foot. I was working up a colossal rage. You just walked right into the middle of it."

"What are you so angry at, if not the quack grass?"

He narrowed his eyes at her. "You're serious, aren't you? You think because I'm a little annoyed, I'm sick of ranching. You're just holding your breath waiting for me to take a false step so you can say, see, he hates it here, and marry your precious lawyer without guilt." Saige kicked a dirt clod, shattering it to dust. "Well, it isn't going to happen."

"So..." Lily looked at the tractor, she stared at the row of pines at the edge of the field, she gazed down at the dirt she'd gotten in her sandals. "So if you're not bored with ranching, you must be...already bored with me?" She made it a question.

Saige roared a sibilant oath at the top of his voice. "Bored? I'm crazy, not bored! Aggravated, bored, restless. Do you have any other halfhearted words for it, Blue? What I am is in constant furious torment at the anguish you're going to cause yourself, and me, if you marry that iceman and produce—'' his whole body tightened ''—his *children* to run around Deep Water driving me mad with grief.''

"He's not an iceman," Lily said weakly.

Saige's tone softened. "I know I hurt you, Blue. I'll pay for it every day for the rest of my life. But you—'' he punctuated his words with jabs at the air ''—are going to ruin yours marrying him.''

"You don't give Randall enough credit," Lily said. "He helped me a lot. You wouldn't have been glad to come home to me if I'd just sat out at the ranch for seven years turning into a...lump."

"Are you deaf and blind?" Saige grabbed her shoulders and shook her, not hard, not as though he meant it, more like he couldn't help himself. "I'd've been glad, hell, I'd've been eternally grateful, to come home to you any way I could. I love you. I'll love you till my dying breath."

His fingers tightened on her arms, making her wince. Uttering another oath, Saige released her, but only for a second. He grabbed her again, gently, and hugged her tightly against him. But not so tightly, Lily had to admit, that she couldn't pull away if she wanted. Berating herself for finding pleasure in his arms, she listened to the pounding of his heart beneath her ear. Against her better judgment, she felt herself melting.

Saige must have felt it, too, for his rage dissipated. "I hurt you, Blue," he whispered into her hair. "But I never lied to you. I'm not lying now."

I wish I could believe you. Lily groaned to herself. Aloud she said nothing, fearing her voice would give away inner thoughts she wasn't ready to face. She had to get out of this embrace.

Saige's hands moved over her back. "I'll let you go," he said as his hands found the curve of her bottom. "I know they can see us from the road."

"Uh-huh," Lily agreed. "You should let me go."

Neither of them moved.

Saige brought his mouth closer. "Run if you want," he warned. "Now or never."

With all the intestinal fortitude she could muster, Lily commanded her body to move out of his grasp, but it seemed unaware of her orders. Her hands moved up his chest, slightly damp with sweat, hot from the sun and their closeness and their want, to link behind his neck. Her mouth sought his.

Saige locked his lips to hers in a searing kiss, more intense than any they'd shared since his return. The Fourth of July happened all over again as passion exploded in her mind, pounding her heart with the joy of being alive in Saige's arms, of feeling the life in him. The pressure of his lips, the strength of his arms around her swept pleasure through her veins, along every nerve.

His hands moved down her spine, caressing places he knew she craved his touch. His tongue stroked a hauntingly familiar, wildly tantalizing rhythm along the roof of her mouth, making her wonder how she had lived all these years without this delight. She slid her hands down his ribs, around his waist, into the back pockets of his Levi's, gripping the hard muscles in his buttocks.

Bells began to ring. Lily groaned deep in her throat and pulled him closer against her. Saige had created all sorts of delicious feelings in her over the years, but he'd never actually made bells ring before. Nor horns honk.

Horns honk? Lily opened her eyes and pulled back. Horns continued to honk. Merciful heaven, a long chain of cars was driving slowly down the county road, wending its way from the church to a wedding reception.

Surely the horns honked for the bride and groom. Except, Lily noted with dismay as she peeked around Saige's broad shoulders, many of the people driving by were waving out their windows at Saige and Lily in the field.

She ducked behind his protecting body again. Nervously she tried to straighten her hair. "I'm sorry, Saige. I shouldn't have done that."

"You didn't do it, Lily." For once, Saige looked less than proud of having seduced her into passion. "I did it to you."

"You said I could go."

"Sure I did, after I wrapped you up till you couldn't move and yelled at you how much I loved you." He lifted his hat to rake a hand through his hair. "Felt real free to go then, didn't you?"

"Don't, Saige." Lily put a hand on his forearm. "It wasn't your arms that held me. It was—"

"Yeah?" A broad smile split Saige's face, his eyes radiating hope and a flicker of triumph. "It was what, Blue? C'mon, love, tell me."

Lily's eyes widened as she realized what her foolish tongue had been about to utter. With a gasp, she drew back her hand and turned toward her car. Before she could take a step, Saige's long fingers closed around her wrist, and she was facing him again.

"True Blue," he said, his predatory grin reminding her of something between a wolf and a shark. He slid the thumb of his free hand back and forth along her lower lip, still swollen from his kisses. "Open these and talk to me."

Willing her heart to stop its frantic pace, Lily stared at his strong hand surrounding her wrist, restraining her flight. Another car horn sounded, making her realize how they must look to the passing wedding guests—at least one of whom would undoubtedly describe the scene to Randall—as if she held Saige's hand by choice.

She grimaced as she imagined Randall's coming lecture, for she knew she would have trouble defending herself from that charge. Could she really tell Randall honestly that she struggled mightily and Saige refused to let her go? That, of *course*, she had not held his hand of her own free will?

Saige gave another gentle tug on her wrist. "Don't try to hold out on me, love. I know you too well."

A welcome surge of anger hit Lily. "*Me* hold out?" She raised her eyes to his. "You've got a nerve. For all I know, you spent the last seven years with a woman so enthralling you forgot to let me know you'd be a few lifetimes late. Or maybe a whole series of women." Saige dropped her hand as if it burned him. "Don't you dare say *I'm* holding out!"

The dark red of anger suffused his neck. "*I'm* not the one filing for divorce, Mrs. Alexander." He held his hands stiffly at his sides, his shoulders tense. Every line of his body exuded a rage he held barely in check. "*I'm* not the one about to ruin three lives by marrying someone with all the passion of a bowl of oatmeal just because—" Saige's voice could probably be heard in the next county "—I'm too damn scared to take a little risk."

"A *little* risk? You sanctimonious hypocrite! I nearly died last time you left me. Died, do you hear?" Lily had a feeling her words were carrying as far as his. "What do you suppose it will do to me the next time?"

"Next time?" Saige's voice suddenly dropped, becoming uncomfortably, ominously quiet. "I've told you, Lily, there will never be a next time. If you say that to me one more time, woman—" his finger jabbed the air with every word "—so help me, I'll—I'll..." A gleam came into his narrowed gaze as he eyed her backside. "I'll—"

Deciding she had no desire to learn exactly what mayhem Saige could dream up, Lily fled.

After a sleepless weekend, Lily arrived at Randall's office Monday morning, prepared to sign whatever was necessary to get her divorce under way. She didn't want to do it. She knew it would hurt as much as anything she'd done since Saige left her.

But she'd spent thirty-six sleepless hours mulling over her anguish and knew this was the right thing to do. Saige's outburst in the field reminded her too intensely of his speeches about adventure just before he left for South America. His swearing at the quack grass reminded her even more of the myriad responsibilities of ranching that had always bored him silly in the past.

Love meant more than kissing. She loved to kiss Saige, she admitted it. She even loved to dream about him settling down and becoming a responsible husband and father. But she'd had that dream before, and it had turned into a nightmare. No matter what he said, Saige was running too true to form for her to believe in his transformation into a small-town rancher.

If she made the mistake of trusting him again, and he again broke her trust, she wouldn't just stop loving him, she'd hate him. If they had a child then, she'd hate her child's father. She couldn't take that risk, not when she'd bet her last penny that the risk was a sure thing.

Randall loved her and she loved him. True, it wasn't the sparks-flying kind of love she used to feel for Saige. With Saige home, Lily couldn't help recognizing that. But she was older now. She could live without feeling her heart leap in her chest every time she saw her husband.

That sort of intensity didn't last, she'd learned that. It was a girlhood dream and belonged in the attic of her mind, along with Saige's dream of traveling the world.

Randall's secretary had not arrived yet, and Lily opened the door to his inner office. He rose from behind his desk, tension deepening the lines in his face. Guilt assailed her for causing him to suffer because of her indecision.

She went to him and kissed his cheek. He responded almost desperately, clutching her hard and returning the kiss.

"My sweet," he murmured into her hair. "You've made up your mind?"

"Yes," she said. "I knew before, I just had to be sure."

Randall slid into his chair and pulled her onto his lap, kissing her harder than ever. "My dear girl," he said. "We'll file the divorce petition today."

Lily had readied herself. She didn't even flinch at his words.

CHAPTER NINE

LILY woke to darkness. For days it had nagged at the edges of her consciousness, and for days she had ignored it. But now, in the night, with nothing to distract her, her mind forced her to picture again exactly what she'd seen in Randall's bedside table drawer the night he'd nearly taken her to bed: a box of condoms, open and tipped over, spilling its contents. She could see the packets scattered around the drawer as clearly now as she'd seen them that night. And she could count only seven.

Seven! Didn't they come in boxes of twelve? And three? Yes, she'd seen three packs advertised in *Cosmo* since the AIDS virus started. But not seven.

Seven could mean only one thing. Randall had used some.

Suddenly finding the darkness too intense, Lily sat up and reached for the lamp. In the light she'd see something more substantial than images on her mind: the photograph of her and Randall at their engagement party, the double wedding ring quilt he'd bought for her at the craft fair last

Thanksgiving. Anything to get rid of the memory of him slamming the drawer as she gazed into it.

They hadn't been formally engaged all that long, she reminded herself, less than a year, in fact. But three years before that Randall had professed his love for her and begun asking her to marry him.

Lily threw off the covers and wandered into the living room. Until the other night, she hadn't really understood how intensely Randall felt about the physical side of love. Guilt assailed her as she realized how selfish she'd been expecting such a sacrifice from him.

Yet she'd demanded it of herself. And it hadn't been easy. Many times she'd lain awake, remembering Saige's touch so profoundly she'd almost cried aloud. The day after such tormented nights, she'd always clung desperately to Randall, longing to have him make her one with him.

But something had stopped her. Something inside had refused to let her make false promises to two men. She had to revoke the commitment she'd made to one before she could promise faithfulness that meant anything to another. For seven years she had felt that way. She felt that way tonight.

But, she had to face it, she had assumed too much about Randall. *He* had made no commitments to anyone. He had believed Saige dead and now found him an unbelievably vexing, ill-timed thorn in his side. Because Randall loved her, he'd understood her reluctance and made no sexual demands. But he hadn't promised to forsake anything and wouldn't until they made their marriage vows.

So why did she care? Why did she feel betrayed and hurt? Why did she want to call him now, at three in the morning?

In the light spilling from her bedroom, Lily found her way to the kitchen phone and dialed Randall's number. It rang and rang. Finally she heard the sound of his receiver clattering to the floor, then his muffled cursing.

"—'Lo," he said groggily.

"Randall, this is Lily."

"Lil'beth," he grunted. "What time is it? Is something wrong?"

"It's three in the morning, and something is wrong." She paused. "Well, no... really nothing's wrong. I mean no one's sick or anything. I just..."

"What is it?" Randall sounded wide awake now.

"I wanted to know what you did with the rest of the condoms," she said. "You know, the ones that had already been used."

A long silence ensued, but Lily had no fears that Randall had gone back to sleep. "I'll be right there," he said at last.

During the ten minutes it took Randall to dress and drive to her apartment, Lily started a pot of tea. She doubted either of them needed coffee to stay awake tonight. The tea hadn't finished steeping when he pounded on her door.

As soon as she opened it, he lunged into the kitchen, grabbing her and hauling her against him. Holding her in a bear hug, he began pressing kisses to her temples, her face, her neck, the top of her head.

"Lillabeth," he groaned against her throat. "I do love you."

"I know you do," she said, thinking she believed it. "But I wish you had told me."

Randall pulled her into the living room. Lowering himself onto the couch, he tugged her onto his lap. "Told you what? That I got so frustrated with desire for you, I could hardly keep from dragging you to my bed? That would have made your grief a lot easier to bear, wouldn't it?"

"I made a vow, Randall. I'll make the same one to you next month." She pulled back and looked at him. "What do you want it to mean to me then?"

He took her face between his palms. "I never questioned your fidelity. I loved it." He kissed her lips. "But it's different for a man."

"Different?" Lily cried. Of all the things Randall could have said, that hurt the worst. "Do you think it was easy for me?"

"Easier than for me, sweetheart. Women don't understand what it does to a man." He cleared his throat. "It's why you were able to remain faithful to Saige, even when you were falling in love with me. You just don't have the same needs as a man."

"How can you believe that?"

"Darling," Randall said. "Those women meant nothing to me. I never gave them my love."

"Is that supposed to make me feel better?" Lily pushed herself off his lap.

"And there've been none..." Randall looked away from her penetrating gaze. "Really...none since our engagement. Before that, my dear, we made no commitments to each other."

Lily went to the kitchen and poured two cups of tea with shaking hands. When Randall tried to embrace her from behind, she turned and pushed a mug into his hands. "What kind of commitment do you plan to make to me at our wedding, Randall? Will it mean *anything*?"

"It will mean everything, Lillabeth." He slammed his mug onto the counter. "More than simple fidelity. I'll pledge my life to you. Won't that be enough? What more would you like?"

Randall was getting angry. She could hear an edge to his voice he'd never used with her before. He braced his hands on the counter behind her, pinning her between his arms.

"I never promised to act the monk for you, Lillabeth," he yelled. "I think it's damned unreasonable of you to expect it."

Lily tried to move away, but the counter shoved into her back. "Why didn't you tell me you couldn't wait?"

"What good would that have done?" he snarled.

Lily looked at the infuriated face looming over her. "I wouldn't have spent years in blissful ignorance, Randall. I would have understood how much I was asking of you."

"Big deal, my sweet," Randall said, his voice dripping sarcasm. "Would it have made you divorce your long-lost husband to marry me?"

"Of course it might," Lily said quietly. "I never wanted you to suffer."

Randall seemed to deflate. His stiff shoulders slumped. His confining arms slid off the counter and hung at his sides.

"Oh, God," he muttered, turning away.

Lily gazed despondently at his back. "I've spent years pouring out all my woes to you. Did you think me so shallow I wouldn't listen to yours?"

Randall spun around. "Never shallow. Just so fragile. At first, you know, you were. I didn't notice how strong you've become." He pulled her against him, pushing her head under his chin.

"This just makes our relationship seem . . . so false."

"That's not true!" he said. "I only meant to protect you."

"Protect me?" she said. "Not a way I'd have chosen."

"Perhaps not," Randall said. "But that was my purpose." He took her and held her away from him. "This all happened years ago, Lillabeth. At a time when you were still reminding me daily that you loved your missing husband so desperately that you'd never take another. Do you know what that did to me?"

"Oh Randall, I—"

"Lillabeth, please give me—give us—another chance."

As he tried to pull her close again, Lily put a hand against his chest. "I can't just go on as if nothing has happened, Randall. I feel...betrayed."

"I never betrayed you, Lillabeth," Randall insisted, a pleading note in his voice. "Please don't do anything rash. Think about this, I beg you."

Lily stared at Randall's crumpled shirt, his dress slacks without a belt. She had never seen him so disheveled. He must have dressed in moments to hurry over here so fast. Obviously he cared deeply for her—in his own way.

Her feelings were less clear to her. "I need some time, Randall. Alone. I need to think—"

"Of course," he agreed hurriedly. "I understand. I won't call you for a week."

"Two," she amended.

"Till the rodeo?" Randall said. "Very well, but..." He hesitated, then spoke in his most lawyerly voice. "You do mean alone? You...we won't see other people during this time."

"You mean, am I going to fling myself into Saige's arms?" Lily asked dryly. "Believe me, this has nothing to do with Saige. I need to think about us." She gave him a hard stare. "What about you, Randall? Can you wait a few weeks? Or am I asking too much again?"

"Of course I'll wait." Randall grabbed her and squeezed her till she thought she couldn't draw a breath. "I don't deserve you, Lillabeth. But I don't want anyone else."

Lily sat in her window seat, staring out the bay window, waiting for the dawn. Randall had left, pleading exhaustion, but she couldn't sleep.

All these years, she'd been so sure of him. Now he'd shown her a side of himself she never knew existed. She couldn't help wondering if there were other sides she didn't know, either. She'd known him six years. How many other secrets did he withhold from her?

The sky brightened, lightening Lily's mood. She glanced at her watch and at the sky. Just after five o'clock. A month ago dawn would have come much earlier. Still, she mused, plenty of time for a ride.

Her heart fluttered. A dawn ride? She hadn't ridden in the morning since Saige left. They used to ride together before Grace and Warren got up. She'd suggested it once to Randall, but he hadn't wanted to interfere with the cowboys that early and said his Lamborghini would wake up all the guests.

Saige's visit last week, his offer of her old horse and privacy on the ranch, had put the idea in her head, and she couldn't get it out. Before Lily's conscious mind had resolved to do it, her subconscious had led her into the bedroom to don riding clothes.

She parked her car on the ranch road, a quarter of a mile from the house, so as not to awaken Saige. When she walked into the yard, nothing stirred. Thank heavens Invictus wasn't taking a morning prowl.

She entered the barn and in the darkness instinctively reached for bridles where they had always hung. Several felt dry and cracked, but two were smooth and supple. Saige had oiled them, hers as well as his. He must have guessed she wouldn't be able to resist a ride on Serendipity.

At the corral, Lily climbed the fence. Serendipity and Virago grew still, watching her with what? Suspicion or curiosity? Did this early morning visit rouse old memories for them as it did for her? Serendipity, a beautiful sorrel thoroughbred, pranced toward her a few steps, cocking her large fine-boned head curiously. Virago stepped in front of her as if protecting her from Lily.

Lily made cooing sounds, and Serendipity's head snapped up. The mare walked toward her, pushing past Virago to get to the fence. Lily stroked her neck, rubbing her cheek against Serendipity's coat.

"Atta girl," Lily murmured. "Don't let men—" she giggled "—especially gelded ones tell you what to do."

She slipped the bridle over Serendipity's head and stroked the length of the mare's back, down her flanks. "You're as beautiful as ever, girl. We don't need that old saddle, do we?"

Holding the bridle, Lily climbed the fence and mounted the bare back of her thoroughbred, sliding into position just behind Serendipity's withers. She sat still a moment, savoring the feeling of the horse's warmth beneath her legs.

She'd never ridden her quarter horse bareback. Randall didn't think it safe. And perhaps she hadn't really wanted to, hadn't wanted to risk dredging up these memories of early morning rides with her husband.

Suddenly and piercingly, Lily knew why she had named her quarter horse Sera. She had feared, so deeply she couldn't explain it, giving up all remembrance of her old life, her old love, casting it and him out of her mind as if it had never existed. No matter if it was gone and could not be retrieved; it had existed, it was part of her.

Serendipity pranced sideways, eager to run.

"You do remember, don't you, girl?" Lily asked, almost laughing with glee at the rush of freedom she felt. With a flick of her heels, she urged the horse toward the gate. She leaned down and pulled back the latch. "You know where we're going, don't you girl?"

"Sure she does," Saige said.

Lily brought her gaze up with a jerk. Saige pulled open the gate and waited, one hand on the gate, one hand stuffed negligently in the pocket of his jeans. He wore no shirt, his jeans were zipped but not snapped, and somehow she knew he hadn't put on socks before tugging on his old boots. In fact, she had a good idea he hadn't put much on beneath the jeans, either.

She stared into his gray-green eyes and felt her lips pulling into an answering smile despite herself. "Don't come with us."

"Not on your tintype." His tousled hair hung into his brow, sleep lingered in his heavily lidded eyes, and he hadn't shaved. "Three's a crowd." He patted Serendipity's rump as she passed him.

Saige's appearance shattered the total ease Lily had felt moments ago. But knowing his gaze lingered on her as she started down the ranch road added to her exhilaration. Nothing would stop her from enjoying this ride.

Her excitement must have translated itself to the horse. Serendipity took only a few walking steps before breaking into a lope. In a saddle, Lily always needed time to adjust to her horse's gait. Not bareback. The horse's backbone felt like a part of her own skeleton. She and Serendipity were one being, and none of the animal's movements surprised her.

Near where Lily had parked her car, Serendipity leaped a small ditch into the freshly mowed hay field and burst into a gallop across the windrows. Leaning low over her neck, Lily tangled her hands into Serendipity's mane and let the horse go. As they picked up speed, Lily threw back her head and shouted at the top of her voice.

Serendipity chose their path, sometimes jumping bales, sometimes dodging them. The wind in Lily's face made tears stream from her eyes, and the smell of fresh cut grass tantalized her. Things beside her began to blur. She saw only Serendipity's lush brown mane twisting through her fingers, felt the massive muscles bunching and stretching beneath her thighs.

She belonged here. Despite the flying pace of her mare, Lily had no fear. Serendipity belonged here, too. She remembered the way as well as Lily. The mare's warmth turned to heat, and the smell of horse sweat rose. Lily breathed hard, and Serendipity panted beneath her. Finally the animal began to slow.

Lily lifted her head and brushed tears off her cheeks. Far out on the highway, cars drove downhill toward town. She didn't need to look at her watch to know her riding time had come to an end.

She turned Serendipity toward the barn, jumping one last bale. As she left the field, she saw Saige, leaning against her car, his arms crossed over his hair-matted chest. At his feet,

Invictus twisted a figure-eight path in and around Saige's ankles, rubbing his furry back against the soft old boot leather.

Reaching up, Saige grasped the reins near Serendipity's head. "I'll take her."

"You don't need to do that."

He raised a brow. "After what you said about private meetings, I figure you want to get out of here before anyone shows up to work."

Lily nodded, smiling, still tingling with excitement. "You're probably right." Her gaze flicked toward the highway again and reality hit her. "As if that's going to do a bit of good, Saige Alexander, and you know it." She shook a finger at him as if it was his fault. "When I turn my car onto that highway from this road, at this hour..." All her desire to smile vanished. Within hours of promising Randall that she would spend their time apart alone—not with Saige—she was going to be seen leaving Saige's ranch. "What will Randall think when he hears?"

Saige made no effort to hide his amusement. "I know what *I'd* think if I saw you leaving *his* place at six-thirty in the morning." He aimed a thumb toward the house. "If you'd like to make the rumor true, I'd be happy to oblige."

Lily didn't bother to respond to his innuendo. "What do you think my chances are of getting back to town without seeing anyone?"

Saige shrugged, his grin undimmed. "About seven hundred to one."

She cocked her head. "How did you come up with that figure?"

"That's the population of Deep Water. One of 'em's bound to see you." He chuckled without rancor. "I'm not the one who got you into this mess this time, Lily." He stretched his hands to her waist and lifted her from the horse. "But I'm glad I got to watch."

Reins in hand, he turned and headed toward the corral. She dragged her eyes away from his half-naked body and climbed into her car. Horse hair covered her legs, and sweat stuck her T-shirt to her back. Oh, the heck with both these men—*she* felt wonderful! As she backed the car around, Lily began to laugh.

When Randall found out, as he surely would, he would no doubt lecture and act disappointed. Perhaps he'd even shout and behave threateningly as he had last night. She didn't care. She needed this, and she would do it again.

CHAPTER TEN

LILY drove her car behind the weathered gray rodeo arena, wondering as she always did how much longer the old wooden structure could stand. She drove more slowly than even the bumpy rutted track required, for she had to stop frequently to avoid horses ridden and led, children and parents done up in Western garb they never wore the rest of the year, and hawkers of programs and peanuts and soda.

Every time she stopped, someone chatted with her through her open window, agreeing that this rodeo was more fun than the real one on the fourth, and wasn't it a beautiful day? Not nearly as hot as a month ago, which would be better for the kids and the horses, though 4-H wouldn't sell as much lemonade.

Lily parked and took out her camera. As she walked behind horse trailers, getting shots of parents helping groom and saddle horses and fuss with their kids' attire and of nervous, excited kids trying to keep their animals calm, she wondered how anyone could say this wasn't a real rodeo.

Lily arrived at the large area set aside for Kokie's camp, a ring formed by six large horse trailers, each bearing the C Bar Three brand. Randall's yellow Lamborghini was parked off to the side, safely behind the trailers.

Snapping pictures, Lily tensed at the sight. This would be the first time she'd seen Randall since their agreement to spend time apart. Though she knew he had too much good breeding and reserve to discuss their relationship here, she couldn't help worrying about this meeting.

"Darling." Randall appeared next to her, giving her shoulders his familiar camera-jostling hug and her cheek a friendly peck. "I'm so glad you made it to the rodeo." He couldn't have been more natural. "You'll be glad, too. Mother's nearly beside herself with excitement. We have a real chance this year." His voice quivered with enthusiasm.

Relaxing at Randall's obvious pleasure at seeing her again, Lily returned his quick kiss. She had missed him, too, she realized. Perhaps she had overreacted—a bit—to his indiscretions. After all, that had all happened years ago. Surely she should forgive Randall for long-past sins.

"You were right about Saige," Randall went on as if they had seen each other yesterday.

"I was?" Lily asked, stunned to hear him sound so magnanimous about Saige. This was the old Randall, the one she had known the last six years.

"Alexander has his faults, but the kids love him, Crysta especially. Wait until you see her and her partner in the ribbon race." Randall's face glowed. "If they come in first, as we expect, it'll be Mother's first blue ribbon for the camp."

"What do you mean, all the kids?" Lily asked from behind her camera. "I thought he was only teaching Crysta."

"Didn't you know he's been working with the rest of the children?" Randall asked.

Lily stopped peering through her lens long enough to frown at Randall. "Of course not, Randall. Just as you asked, I haven't gone to the dude ranch since you and your mother ganged up on me."

"Now, dear," Randall said, his tone patronizingly indulgent. "That's a little strong, isn't it? Besides, you were happier staying away from Saige."

"Just tell me about the horse camp," Lily said impatiently.

"Saige worked with Crysta for a week or so. Since then he's coached all the children. Every day." Randall grabbed Lily's elbow and moved her as a cowboy led a C Bar Three horse down the ramp. "He's been quite...faithful." He mumbled the last word as if admitting such a thing about Saige troubled him.

"Faithful? You mean responsible, conscientious, reliable?" Lily watched Randall's chagrin grow with each adjective and wondered if she was teasing him or herself. "All those words never uttered in the same breath with the name Saige Alexander?"

"Well, yes, my dear," Randall finally said, with a shrug. "I suppose that's exactly what I'd call him. And not only that. He helped our camp more than the working cowboys ever could." He waved a hand toward several of the cowboys unloading horses and gear. "Saige hadn't their other duties, so he devoted himself entirely to the children, and they love him."

A moment later, Randall's words proved prophetic as the C Bar Three bus, an old school bus done up to look like a stage coach, arrived with Saige driving and all twelve of the camp kids waving out the window. As soon as he stopped, they poured out, seeking their horses and equipment.

Saige left the bus last and was immediately surrounded by children, tugging at his hands and his belt, pulling him toward their horse and their saddle for his help and approval. Lily gawked as Saige went patiently from child to child and horse to horse, giving almost no help but lots of admiration and hugs.

Lily swallowed and realized her jaw hung slack. She'd never seen Saige with children before, except that one afternoon with Crysta. Here, with the kids so excited and eager for his attention, he resembled the Pied Piper. What had made her think he didn't want children? He looked more content than any time she'd seen him since his return.

"No!" Crysta suddenly screamed, attracting all their attention. She backed away from Kokie, palms out. "No, ma'am, I won't. If I can't ride Sera, I ain't ridin'."

Saige quickly stepped behind Crysta, putting both his hands on her shoulders and holding her protectively in front of him. Lily and Randall joined the group a second later. All three obviously wished to cool one side or the other of what was becoming a heated argument between Crysta and Kokie.

Shorty stood nervously to one side, holding the reins of a jittery black gelding named Skeezix. Lily had ridden Skeezix several times and had never seen him behave so badly. She was sure Crysta's crying and shrieking increased the horse's nerves.

Crysta slid to the side of Saige's body and wrapped her arms around his waist. "I ain't," she shouted. "I ain't ridin'. I only ride Sera. I ain't ridin' him. I can't."

"Yes, indeed, you will, young lady," Kokie said snappishly. "We cannot permit this sort of outburst here. You're upsetting the animals and the other children. I'm sure you can be heard at the ticket booth."

Saige stroked Crysta's hair, making no effort to dislodge her grip around her middle. "It's okay,

Crysta. You don't have to ride unless you want to." He glanced at Shorty. "Where's Sera?"

"Pulled up lame this morning," Shorty said. "Didn't have time to do nothing about it before we headed out. Doc said he'd check her after the rodeo."

"I ain't ridin'," Crysta said adamantly, her tears replaced by stubbornness now that she had Saige's backing.

"Young lady," Randall began in a tone so severe Lily's eyes widened at him. Crysta ducked behind Saige's body and peeked at Randall. "Mrs. Carver spent a great deal of money for you to learn to ride a horse and enjoy a vacation your parents couldn't possibly provide. She asks nothing in return except that you perform your best at this rodeo."

Saige pulled Crysta from behind him but kept his arm firmly around her shoulders. "She doesn't have to ride, Carver. She doesn't owe you or your mother a damn thing."

"She most certainly does," Kokie put in peremptorily. "I made it quite clear to these participants from the first day that their goal was to ride for the C Bar Three in the rodeo. They all agreed. This young lady agreed." She narrowed her eyes at Crysta. "Didn't you, Crystal?"

"My name's Crysta," she said, sticking out her lower lip. "An' I only ride one horse."

"You can win, Crysta," Kokie said. "My son has told me how well you ride the ribbon race. I'd like to see you win."

"Not on that horse, I can't."

Randall grabbed Crysta's arm, his patience clearly at an end. "Just mount the horse," he said. "Perhaps you won't have any trouble." He tried to tug her toward the horse.

"No!" shrieked Crysta, wrapping her arms around Saige again.

"Good God, Carver," Saige said, grabbing Randall's wrist and forcefully removing his grip from Crysta's arm. "What do you want to do? Hurt her? Or just injure the horse?" He stepped back with Crysta glued to his side and glared at Randall. "Use your brains. If you've got any."

By that time, all the other kids and most of the cowboys had gathered around the arguing group. Saige's last remark brought forth a chorus of nervous giggles. Dark red suffused Randall's neck and face.

"Crysta Johnson," he roared, his rage nearly palpable. "You get on that horse now."

Saige tightened his arm around the girl. "You don't have to, Crysta."

Crying, she released Saige's comfortable waist. "I got to, I guess."

Saige hunkered down to her height. "Not unless *you* want to."

Crysta took a breath full of tears. "I guess I got to try."

Terror glittered in her large dark eyes as Crysta moved toward Skeezix with Saige right behind her. The horse, unused to raised voices and contention, now appeared as high-strung as an unwilling racehorse being shoved into a starting gate. He jumped away from Crysta twice as she tried to mount.

"Saige," Crysta wailed.

Looking grim, Saige took the reins from Shorty and stroked Skeezix several times, speaking soothing words to the animal. Keeping his voice calm and steady, he mounted the horse and rode him away from the cluster of children down the dusty rodeo road. In a few minutes, he returned on the easygoing Skeezix Lily knew.

Dismounting, he beckoned to Crysta and hunkered down to her height. Together they stroked Skeezix's neck. "Only if you want to, Crysta," he repeated.

Crysta didn't say a word, just nodded. With a glower over her head for Kokie and Randall, Saige picked her up and put her on the horse's back.

When Crysta took the reins from Saige, fright made her motions too quick and jerky. She wrenched at the bit in Skeezix's mouth, and he fought her, snorting and dancing sideways several quick steps. Crysta screamed and dropped the reins to clutch the saddle horn. Lily's heart shot to her throat as Skeezix reared.

Saige lunged for the reins and pulled the horse down. With a disgusted oath at Randall, or possibly himself, he lifted Crysta out of the saddle.

"Go sit in the stands and watch, honey," he said. "You don't have to ride."

"I'm very disappointed in you, Crysta," Kokie said. "I thought you would make us all proud today."

"Leave her alone, Kokie!" The furious words burst from Lily before she could stop them.

"Randall," Kokie snapped. "I will not tolerate such treatment from your fiancée. Please make that clear to her." With an angry look that included everyone in sight, she swept out of the enclosure.

Crysta sobbed against Saige's jeans once more. "I want to go home," she cried.

"C'mon," he said. "I'll take you."

"No, Saige, no," cried a dozen young voices. "Stay. Watch me. You said you'd watch us ride."

Saige looked helplessly at Lily. She had never felt so eager to do anyone a favor. She didn't think she could stay in Randall's presence another second without exploding.

Lily understood what Saige didn't, that Kokie would give up her pearl and emerald dinner ring to have one of her city kids win a blue ribbon at the rodeo. The city kids had slim hope of ever beating their competition, ranch kids who rode every day of their lives, and regular summer kids who rode every day of the summer. Crysta was the first real hope the camp had ever had.

Nonetheless, Lily wanted to slap Randall and Kokie silly. How *dare* they risk an injury to one of the children in their care? She couldn't believe it. Nausea roiled in her stomach at the memory of Crysta's terrified shriek atop Skeezix. What if Saige hadn't gotten to her in time?

Lily leaned down to Crysta. "I'll take you home, honey," she whispered. "C'mon. Just the two of us." She stroked the little girl's back.

Crysta transferred her hug to Lily's neck. "I'm sorry."

"What for?" Lily asked. "*You* didn't do anything wrong."

"I was awful."

"You were *not*," Lily said. She leaned close to Crysta's ear. "Let's go get an ice cream and we can talk about who was really awful."

Crysta made a sniffling, giggling noise. "You kiddin'?"

"No, I'm serious."

Randall expelled a gusty breath. "Lillabeth, who is going to take pictures of the rodeo?"

She straightened up and narrowed her eyes at him. "I couldn't care less, Randall."

He looked stunned at her tone. "But . . . but we always send home photos of the kids on horseback for their parents."

Lily bit her lip. She wanted to throw her camera right in Randall's startled face. But she didn't want to disappoint the other kids, who would probably love to take home a record of their equestrian feats. Most of all, however, she wished not to submit to Randall's orders in front of all these people after he'd behaved so abominably.

Turning to Saige, Lily put the camera in his hands, carefully wrapping his long fingers around it. "Since you seem to have brains that work today, do you think you can manage this?"

Saige showed the restraint not to smile, but amusement danced in his eyes. "I think I can handle it, Mrs. Alexander."

Randall sputtered behind her at Saige's use of her married name. Lily pursed her lips at Saige, refusing to laugh or even smile. "Very well. C'mon, Crysta."

Without a glance at Randall, Lily led Crysta to her car. Beating sun had turned the inside to an oven, and they stood outside for a moment after opening the doors to let the interior cool. Crysta stood stiffly, not saying a word, shooting glances over her shoulder at her camp mates— and Randall.

When they got inside the car at last, she let out a huge breath as if she had been holding it. "Man," she said. "That horse scared the sh—" She clamped her lips shut and stared at the floorboards.

"Scared the, er, pudding out of you, Crysta?" Lily suggested.

"Yeah, right. Pudding." Crysta leaned back against the seat and seemed to shrink as tension flowed out of her. "Don't tell 'em I said that. The counselor in San Diego, she told us over and over how we couldn't talk that way up here."

"You've had kind of a hard time here, haven't you?"

"Naw," Crysta said. "Only the first day and today. After Saige came, it was ba-ad."

"Bad?"

"No, ba-ad." Crysta gave her patient look. "You know—good. I'd a' come back if they'd let me. Course, they won't let me now."

"They usually don't let any kids come a second time, Crysta." Lily gave her a sympathetic glance. "There are too many others who want to come a first time."

"I know that. But Saige said I could come again next year." She aimed the air-conditioning vent toward her face. "He said I could come to *his* ranch and work and he'd pay me and I could ride all the time."

"*Next* year?" Lily stammered.

"Next summer. Said he'd talk to my mama." Crysta looked at her curiously. "Don't you think he meant it?"

"If he said it, Crysta, I'm sure he meant it." Lily managed to get the words out, but she felt as if they would choke her. She wished Crysta had chosen someone else, *anyone* else, to ask if Saige could be counted on for the long term.

" 'Course now the Carvers won't let him."

Lily was on firmer ground now. "Trust me, Crysta. If Saige wants to ask you up here, Randall and Kokie won't have a thing to say about it."

"You sure?"

"About that?" Lily laughed. "I've never been more sure of anything in my life."

"Good," said Crysta with heavy satisfaction. "Then I'll win a ribbon next year for Saige, not—" she snorted "—that pink-haired old witch."

Lily didn't waste breath admonishing Crysta, since at the moment she entirely agreed with the sentiment. Instead she was overcome with envy at the confidence in the little girl's voice. How could Crysta, a ten-year-old who'd only known him six weeks, feel so sure of Saige's constancy when Lily, who'd loved him for twenty-three years, felt nothing but skepticism?

Loved him for twenty-three years?

Lily's fingers tightened around the wheel till her knuckles turned white. Had she actually thought such a thing? No, thought was much too lucid a word for what her brain was doing just now. Had she allowed such a notion to pass through her mind? She didn't believe it.

She *wouldn't* believe it.

Abruptly, Lily changed the subject to chocolate malteds and California hairstyles. Crysta had already been through far too much today to even notice that Lily nearly hit the ticket booth on their way out of the rodeo grounds.

* * *

Monday morning, Lily sat at her desk glaring at the list of winners she'd just gotten over the phone from the chairman of the Children's Rodeo Committee. With a mental sigh, she turned to her computer, resigned to writing the kind of story she hated. No emotion, no fun, no smell of the dust or cheers from the stands, no joy from the winners or tears from the losers. Just the facts: the rodeo was Saturday, these were the winners. Since she hadn't seen any of the events, she had no choice.

Of course, she *did* have Saige's pictures.

He'd been so excited to see the results of his handiwork with her camera, he'd arrived at her apartment early yesterday morning, insisting on joining her in the darkroom. She had tried to talk him out of it, promising to call him the moment the pictures were printed. But he'd been adamant.

"Not a chance, Lily," he said at her back door, grinning that roguish grin of his. "No darkroom, no film." His long fingers folded possessively around the three small film canisters he'd been holding out to her.

"Saige Alexander," she snapped. "You give me that film. I'm already in enough trouble with Randall."

"For what?" Saige asked innocently. "Telling him the truth for once?"

"What do you mean, the truth?" Lily exclaimed. "I said awful things to him in front of all those kids. And I've never spoken to Kokie that way."

"Then it's about time you did," Saige said. "And the great truth you imparted to dear old Randall was that brains and a heart are worth more than money." His voice gentled and grew husky as he stroked the soft side of his index finger down her cheek. "Remember, Blue, I married you. I know you care a lot more about love than wealth."

"Saige," she begged, weakening to even this briefest of caresses. "Please don't do this to me."

Pain flickered in his eyes, but he withdrew his finger, and for a moment Lily thought she'd won. She should have known better.

Saige put his hands behind him. "If you're worried about propriety, you can tie both my hands behind my back. But I'm *going* to watch these pictures come to life or—" he gave her his Dracula grin again "—no one will."

Gritting her teeth, Lily wondered if she could possibly spend hours alone in the newspaper office with Saige without at least one person, and thus ultimately Randall, finding out about it. But she already knew the answer. As Saige had said a few weeks ago, nothing that happened in Deep Water remained private for long.

She glared at him. He wore a soft blue denim shirt open at the neck, open far enough to show golden hair glistening on his chest. She had to fight twin urges to curl that hair around her fingers or to button his shirt up tight enough to strangle him.

The innocent look he gave her didn't fool her for a second. He knew how much she'd always loved the masculine feel of that curly hair as she ran her palms down the muscular washboard of his abdomen.

With a shuddery breath, Lily brought her mind to the darkroom. Spending the morning there with Saige could kindle more than mere gossip.

Saige let his gaze slide toward the river. "Since you don't want me in the darkroom, would you care to join me on the bridge where I can dispose of these?" He let his fingers open for an instant than curled them shut again as Lily grabbed for her film. "River's pretty high for August, I hear."

"That's my film, you bully."

"Finders, keepers," Saige said, chuckling. "Or maybe I mean, possession is nine-tenths of the law." He feigned a look of sincere curiosity. "Do you know a lawyer we could ask?"

"Oh, all right!" Lily capitulated angrily. "Bring the darn film."

Obviously Saige didn't give a damn what Randall thought or how annoyed he got with Lily. For that matter, if Randall got so angry he broke off the engagement, Saige would rejoice. It didn't take an intimate knowledge of Saige Alexander to see that trying to talk him out of this would only waste Lily's breath.

Slamming her back door, Lily strode down her walk past Saige. Maybe she'd have the blackmailing rat in the darkroom with her, but she didn't have to talk to him. And no matter what Randall and the local gossips thought, she'd have no trouble keeping her distance when she was this mad at him.

Besides, it was long past time, Lily realized, for her to make clear to Randall that being his fiancée, or his wife, did *not* mean she would be his obedient, pliable underling, incapable of independent thought. And when Randall asked her this time how hard she had tried to talk Saige out of his demand that she go off alone with him, she could say emphatically, "very hard," without a flicker of guilt.

She was sure she could.

Lily flicked a glance over her shoulder. Saige followed a few steps behind her, openly admiring her derriere as she walked. Lily stopped abruptly, waiting till his steps brought him beside her. Thank heavens, she thought disgustedly, they'd be working in the dark, where the sight of each other's bodies wouldn't tantalize them.

The next two and half hours turned out to be some of the longest of Lily's life. Though Saige kept his promise not to caress her, the tiny space they worked in made it almost impossible not to touch.

Several times she had to grab his hand to keep him from dumping the wrong chemicals into the stop-bath solutions. With the lights out, the clean male scent of his morning shower mingled with the acid, and she could never be sure where he stood. Again and again their bodies brushed against each other, till Lily wanted to groan with sexual awareness.

Once, when she carried a tray of water to the table and her hands began to shake from proximity to him, he had to wrap his arms around her from behind to steady her. A throbbing began low in her belly, and her breasts felt heavy and swollen from the pressure of his arms beneath them. She longed to throw the water in his face and run from the darkroom, but she had to get her work done.

When she saw the last picture emerge through the developing solution, Lily wanted to cry. "Saige," she said, "didn't you take any others?"

In the dim red light, Saige regarded her across the developing table. "What others? Kokie and Randall?"

"The other kids," Lily wailed. "The winners! The local kids!"

Saige put down the copy of one of his action shots that he'd been admiring. "They don't want 'em."

Lily frowned in confusion. "*Who* doesn't want them?"

"The camp kids," Saige said. "You asked me to take pictures of them to send home to their parents. They want pictures of themselves, not a bunch of Deep Water kids they'll never see again."

"What about the newspaper? I can't run pictures of Randall's camp kids and no one else. Everyone will think..." She groaned, slapping her palm against the table. "You *know* what everyone would think."

Saige shrugged, not looking a bit remorseful. "As I keep telling you, I'm just a rancher. Journalism is *your* job."

"If I still have a job," Lily snapped. "I can't believe I let you trick me into spending half my Sunday alone with you, at the risk of another huge fight with the man I plan to marry, for nothing!"

Saige's frown was real. "You're being unreasonable, Lily."

"I probably am!" she exploded.

Saige leaned over the table close enough to let her feel his breath as he whispered in her ear. "If you want to give the gossips something to talk about—" the laughter in his voice set her teeth on edge "—I have a suggestion."

Lily pulled back. Her voice shook idiotically when she spoke. "Why didn't you *tell* me these were the only pictures you took?"

"I would if you'd asked," Saige said in a tone so reasonable she wanted to slap him. "Are you all right, love? You seem a little edgy to me. Maybe you need a rest."

Lily grabbed the chain on the light and jerked, plunging them into darkness. Turning on her heel, she strode out of the room. The sound of Saige chuckling behind her did nothing to cool her temper.

On her stormy walk home, she'd been willing to admit to herself that Saige had done exactly what she asked him at the rodeo, and that she was irritated with herself for failing to do her job properly. Aloud she wouldn't admit it to that self-satisfied Saige Alexander until his cat could dance the cha-cha.

Leaving her chair as unobtrusively as possible, Lily slipped a copy of her story on Pen's desk and slunk back to her own. This morning, she'd also admit a few other things to herself: that her emotional state *was* making her overreact to everything, the slightest touches, the gentlest jests. And that the confidence she'd felt about Randall and their relationship when Saige had first returned seemed to have evaporated.

Lily didn't understand it. When she considered how sure she had been about their marriage a few weeks ago, confusion overcame her. What had happened? Most bewildering, the change in her feelings didn't seem to have anything to do with Saige.

Like that condom business. All those women. How many had he taken to bed? Only a small part of Lily's pain over this came from jealousy. Worse was her hurt that he'd done it behind her back, that he hadn't told her how much he wanted the physical side of her love.

Somehow worse than anything was Randall's explanation—that those women meant nothing to him. How could Lily love a man who treated women merely as the means for his own satisfaction? Had he told those women the truth before he bedded them? Or had he led them to believe they had a chance with him?

His behavior at the rodeo, coming on top of his betrayal, had shaken Lily deeply. Was this man she hardly knew the real Randall, or was he still the kind gentle man she'd believed him to be for the past six years? She didn't know. Nor did she know what else he might be hiding from her.

Pen's shadow fell across her desk. Lily glanced up, then wished she hadn't. He looked grim. She flashed him a weak smile and returned her gaze to the intriguing paper-clip chain she was making.

"Yes, Pen?" she asked, not quite able to bring herself to initiate what looked to be an uncomfortable discussion of her story.

"I can only assume that your pictures are so exciting there isn't room on the page for a decent story," Pen said with none of his normal good nature.

Lily hooked another paper clip to the string. "I... Not exactly. I mean, no, no pictures at all."

"No pictures." Pen nodded slowly, though Lily saw it only as a shadow on her desk. He pulled up a chair and sat down. "Lil, I understand you're going through a rough time. I've been patient about your work, which I'm sure you admit has slipped.''

Lily met his gaze, despite the gleam of tears she knew must show in her eyes. "I know. I haven't done the kind of job..." She ran out of words.

"The kind of job I pay you to do?" Pen finished for her, frowning. "What in blazes happened on Saturday? If you couldn't cover the rodeo, why didn't you let me know so I could get someone else? If you need a leave of absence, for God's sake take it before you destroy what I've spent years building up!"

Lily wanted to explain. And she would—as soon as she could speak without crying. She leaned her face in her hands to hide her threatening storm of tears and didn't look up when she heard the door to the office slam open.

"Lillabeth!"

She looked up. Randall planted his palms on her desk and leaned over her. Pen sat across from her, his frown undiminished.

"When I heard—" Randall bit the words out "—that you had been embracing your former husband in a hay field the day before you agreed to divorce him, I naturally gave the story no credence. But now I am informed that the day after you publicly abused me and my mother, you spent several hours closeted with him here in the *Register*'s darkroom." He raised a palm from her desk only to slap it down again in front of her. "What of all this rumor is true?"

"In my darkroom, Lil?" Pen asked. "Then where are the pictures?"

Lily looked at Randall's looming face, ruddy with fury. She shifted her gaze to Pen, but that sight offered little relief. Anger, rather than fury, etched his brow. His normally friendly eyes shone with a strong desire to grill her about her use of the darkroom.

But she couldn't answer either one of them, not with these sobs still caught in her throat. Her jaw ached from holding them back. Her eyes flicked back and forth between her choices, a grilling or an inquisition. No wonder she wanted to cry.

With as little noise as possible, Lily covered her face and burst into tears. Silence fell around her.

Finally Randall touched her hair softly. "Lillabeth?"

She batted his hand away and fled to the ladies' room.

CHAPTER ELEVEN

"LIL?" Pen called, tapping lightly on the door. "Are you all right?"

Lily sniffed back tears and didn't answer.

"Please come out and talk to me," Pen said, all vestige of his earlier irritation gone. "Randall told me what happened at the rodeo. I'm sorry I blew up. If I'd been there, I'd've kissed off the job, too." He paused. "After I punched Carver's lights out."

Lily blew her nose and splashed water in her face before answering. "Thanks, Pen. They..." She opened the door and nearly bumped into him. "They got me so upset I didn't think very straight."

"You thought fine," he assured her. "Even with two men doing their darnedest to drive you crazy, you're still a better reporter than anyone else in the state, as far as I'm concerned."

Lily grinned. "I like it when you're trying to make up, Pen. Apologize some more."

"That's enough," Pen said dryly. "If I boost your ego too much, I'll have to give you a raise." He examined her red eyes. "I meant it about time off, Lil. I think you better take the rest of the week."

"I'd just sit home and brood about this," Lily said. "I'd rather work."

Pen shook his head. "You've put off thinking about it long enough—your wedding's in two weeks. You've got to make up your mind."

"I *have* made up my mind." She winced at the obvious note of uncertainty in her voice. "I decided when Saige first came back."

Pen snorted in disbelief.

"But Randall's your best friend," Lily said. "You've always said so."

"I've also always said you were too good for him." Pen gave her a curious look. "Did you think I was kidding?"

"Yes."

Pen shrugged. "I can't tell you who to marry, Lil. I saw what that son of a bitch, Alexander, did to you. I think you're too good for him, as well. But just because Randall and I have done some male bonding doesn't mean I think you ought to marry him."

"I feel so... secure with him." She bit her lip, searching for the right words. "It's not money. I just always know what will happen with Randall."

"No wonder," Pen said. "You put your life in his hands the last six years. Did exactly what he told you to do."

"But he only told me—"

Pen held up a palm. "I know. He was only trying to help. And he *was* good for you, I'd never deny it. But that doesn't mean you should marry him."

"But he—I—" Lily stuttered, swamped with confusion.

"When you thought no one else would ever mean much to you again, Lil, maybe it didn't matter." Pen gave her a hard look. "It matters now."

"But Saige won't stay here," Lily said, her throat constricting with that old familiar fear that she couldn't seem to shake. "He'll leave again. He always leaves."

"Life doesn't give guarantees, Lil." Pen looked understanding but not very sympathetic. Then he relented. "But I'll give you one, the same one I gave Saige the night we talked. If he ever hurts you like this again, I'll find him wherever he is and throttle him myself."

Lily's heart did a little flip-flop. Till now Pen had assiduously avoided saying a word about that night. "Did he— Did Saige, um, say where he'd been?"

Pen laughed. "He told me you'd ask." He took pity on her. "No, Lil, mostly he talked about you." With a hand on her back, he pushed her toward the front door. "Now get out of here until next Monday." He winced. "Well ... Do you think you could cover the banquet Saturday night?"

"You bet, Pen." She kissed him on the cheek. "Thanks."

Lily left the newspaper office, wishing her feelings for Saige and Randall were as easy to understand as her friendship with Pen. Still, she had a week to sort things out and—

"Blue?"

Holding in a groan of dismay that the solitude she needed had already been invaded, Lily glanced up and found Saige leaning against the hood of his pickup, arms folded across his chest. Gone was that ingenuous cowboy look he'd used with such effectiveness yesterday to tug at her heartstrings and remind her of everything good they'd ever shared.

Today he looked desolate, the way he had in Randall's office the night he came home, when he first found out she was engaged. Before he kissed her and quit believing he'd lost her forever.

"Saige, you look awful."

"Thanks," he said. "You don't look so hot yourself."

Frowning, he took a step toward her, and Lily lowered her gaze. He lifted her chin with the edge of his hand and studied her eyes.

Sadness tightened his lips. "Did I make you cry again, Blue?"

"No," she said firmly. "This time it was Randall and Pen. They make quite a team."

Saige's jaw clenched, relaxed, clenched. "I wouldn't have thought that of Pen." He slid his hand to her cheek. "Maybe I should bomb the newspaper office to let him know how I feel about it."

"He apologized," Lily said, leaning into his palm. "Can't you men think of other ways to solve things? Pen threatened to beat up Randall for me ... and throttle you." She gave a monumental sigh. "That's the trouble, Saige. I feel like I'm on a rack. Stretched and pulled in all directions. By you and Randall, and sometimes even Pen."

Saige took her gently in his arms. Intensely aware that they stood in full view of everyone on Main Street, Lily stiffened, trying momentarily to pull out of the embrace. But after the last few days of conflict, his arms offered a comfort too tempting to resist. Telling herself it was insane, she relaxed against him.

"I won't do it anymore, Blue," he said. "I thought I'd quit already, actually."

"No, you didn't, you big phony."

Saige's chuckle rumbled beneath her cheek. "You're right. I tried to quit twisting your arm, but I can't help it. There's too much at stake." He ran a hand down her hair. "I love you too much to give up."

"See?" she murmured.

"I'll try harder." Saige sighed. "Today, anyway. No pressure. If you'll come with me. I need to talk to you."

With an effort of will, Lily put her hands on Saige's shoulders and pushed herself upright. "About what? Did something happen?" Suddenly her heart turned to lead, and the blood seemed to drain from her head. "You're leaving, aren't you? I knew you wouldn't—"

"No!" Saige roared. He leaned over her, anger coming off him in waves. Anger that troubled her not one whit. "Never. Do you hear me, woman? Never!"

Since Lily planned to spend her life with Randall, and Saige's presence in Deep Water would be a constant irritation, his declaration should have worried her. She decided to wait till later to analyze the wave of relief that swept through her, weakening her knees.

"But you look so...like you lost your best friend."

"Close." A shutter seemed to drop over his eyes. "We need to discuss it, to discuss our finances."

"*Our* finances?" Lily said. "I signed everything over to you."

"Not everything, Lily." He cocked his head at her. "Didn't you read the property settlement? You signed it."

Lily felt heat steal into her cheeks. "I guess I didn't read it very carefully. I trusted Randall to tell me whether to sign."

Saige's lips tilted sardonically. "You didn't read it at all, did you?"

Lily bit her lip. "Not a word." She brushed angrily at the hair falling into her eyes. "Damn it, it hurt too much!"

Saige's grin broadened. "Good. I hope it hurt you like fury."

"You—sadist."

"It hurt me more, Blue," he said. "A thousand times more. And I had to read the damn thing. Make sure your lawyer wasn't putting something over on me."

"Randall wouldn't do that."

"Right." He turned away, his back rigid. "Will you come with me?" His voice sounded strained. "No pressure about us. I just need . . . a friend."

Lily eyed him speculatively, seeing pain in the tight stretch of his shirt across his back. She wanted to rub the tension away, as she used to when he came in from a hard day of ranch work. But she hadn't lost *all* her senses. They still stood on Main Street. Pen was probably watching out the window.

"Where are we going?"

"To look at some cows in the Ruby Valley. FHA's about to foreclose on this guy and he needs to sell his herd."

"You want to talk to me about that?" Lily asked. "Saige, you know more about cows than I do. And if you don't have the money—"

"I'll decide about the herd," Saige interrupted. "I need your help on another decision." He gestured toward the pickup. "Please?"

The sorrow clearly etched on his face tore at Lily. With a nod, she opened the passenger door to climb inside. Invictus, thank heavens, wasn't along.

During the drive, Saige fell silent. Lily rested her head against the seat back and let the familiar countryside soothe her. When he downshifted to turn off the highway onto a gravel road, he gave her knee an instinctive pat.

"I thought you'd forgotten I was here," she said.

"Not a chance," Saige said. "The words just won't come very easy." He turned up a ranch road and parked in back near the barn. "The cows are pastured about half a mile away. Let's walk and talk."

As she climbed through the first barbed wire fence, Lily wished she'd had time to go home and change. She had no stockings to run, but she wore only a gauzy midcalf-length skirt with a light blouse and sandals on her feet.

"Some guys dropped by today," Saige finally began, holding two strands of barbed wire apart for her. "Feds actually, from the Drug Enforcement Agency."

"Feds?" Lily straightened with a jerk, nearly impaling herself on a barb. "Dear heaven, Saige. What did they want with you? Did it have to do with where you've been?" Terror gripped her heart. "They can't—can't make you go away again, can they?"

"No, Blue, no." Saige unsnagged her blouse from the fence and pulled her upright. "Nothing like that. In fact—" his voice grew heavy with sadness "—it's really all over now. It's the end."

Lily kept her hand in his, aching from the hurt she saw in his eyes. "Saige, what friend did you lose?"

Saige's eyes took on a suspicious sheen. "Paco." He clenched his jaw. "For seven years, Lily, Paco was my only friend, my only source of information or conversation. Ultimately he saved my life. He's why I'm here now with you."

"Where is he?"

Saige closed his eyes, and his voice tightened with grief. "He was killed when the DEA raided the *latifundia* where I spent the last seven years."

"Oh, Saige." Lily wrapped her arms around his waist. "I'm so sorry."

She held him a long time, waiting for him to tell her more. His breath came and went in shudders. Finally he pulled free and, without a word, began walking again. Lily followed, aware that he needed time to pull himself together.

When they approached the herd he'd come to examine, Saige waited for her and slid an arm around her waist. "Look at 'em," he said. "They're beautiful."

Lily felt ridiculous talking about cows when she desperately wanted to know more about this Paco and the DEA and the lati-whatever that Saige had mentioned. But she remembered all the nonsensical subjects she'd discussed when she couldn't face talking about her anguish over Saige. She'd waited seven years for this explanation. She could wait a few more minutes.

He walked her toward a group of black cows and their calves. The placid animals seemed to help him find a measure of calm.

"Perfect," he mused almost to himself. "This guy doesn't calve till April, and still they're almost as big as their mamas." He waved his free hand toward the animals. "Uniform, big hindquarters, big bags on the moms. They're perfect." He shook his head. "Too bad."

"Too bad?" Lily asked. "What do you mean? I thought that was good."

"They're too good," Saige explained. "Every rancher in three valleys will bid on them. I won't have a chance."

"So you won't even bid?" Lily asked, dismayed at the thought of Saige giving up so easily.

"Damn right I'll bid!" Saige said. "I just hope I can afford it after I…" He stopped and frowned at her ferociously.

"Saige, talk to me," Lily exclaimed. "Tell me now. Start with why you couldn't tell me before and tell me about where you went and how you spent every minute you were gone and what's a lati—"

Saige pressed his thumb against her lips, cutting off her questions. Glancing around, his gaze came to rest on a depleted haystack beneath a rickety old tin roof structure, and he pulled her over to it. Shoving a couple of bales into seats, he offered her one and sat facing her, where he could continue to hold her hands.

"A *latifundia*," he said, beginning with the most neutral topic, "is a big farm, an estate, given by the government. Lots of them have been in one family for generations. This one was near the border—"

"What border?" Lily asked. "What government? Where were you?"

Saige didn't meet her eyes. "Maraguaya."

"Maraguaya?" she exclaimed. "Saige, you didn't. The government is so corrupt. It's just—"

"Right," Saige said. "Just a front for the drug cartels." He stood abruptly as if unable to sit still. "That reporter I told you about hoped to get proof that this *latifundia* was run by an American expatriot. I don't know—I'll never know where he heard that." His hands clenched convulsively into fists. "I'll never even know if we found the right *latifundia*. But we sure as hell found one well-armed. One minute I could see this big agricultural place with lots of buildings and a landing strip with a few small planes exchanging cargo. The next minute, I saw guns pointed up at us, and the plane started going down way too fast."

"Oh, Saige." Lily rose and gripped his forearm. "You must have been so scared."

"That," he said with no hint of humor, "is an understatement of earthshaking proportions." His gaze left hers to study the rusty roof over her head. "They hauled us out and threw us up against the plane. Then they asked my buddy, in Spanish, if he had taken pictures with the camera. He still had it in his hands. When he said yes, they shot him."

"Shot him? Just like that?" Lily's nails pushed harder into Saige's flesh. "Saige, what did you do?"

Saige covered one of her hands on his arm, trying to ease her grip. "I prepared to die, I guess." He pulled himself free and turned aside, gripping an overhead beam as he stared out at the yellowing hillsides. "Know what saved me, Blue? You'll love this."

"Don't make fun," she cried. She wanted to pound on his back to make him see what his words were doing to her, but her feet felt rooted where she stood. "I won't love this. I hate all of it. And it scares me to death, still, even now, with you here, safe."

He spun around, his face full of remorse. "I know." He pulled her close. "Me, too, actually. That's why it's so hard to talk about it. It hasn't gotten easier with time." His arms held her tightly, tenderly, but his body could not relax. After a moment he let her go. "Do you want me to stop?"

Lily shook her head emphatically. "What saved you?"

"My ranch upbringing." She could tell he wanted to speak lightly, but his quavery voice didn't cooperate. "They asked me something in Spanish I didn't understand. After watching my buddy die, I was too scared to make myself translate. Then this guy, Paco, in broken English asked me if I could fix the plane's engine." He gave her the wobbliest of grins. "It was the same kind of plane the cattleman's association used for crop dusting when I was in high school. I fixed that one plenty of times. So I said sure."

Saige's eyes moved restlessly over the herd of cows, which no longer seemed able to calm him. "Paco stared at me a long time. Maybe it was only a few seconds, but it seemed like hours. Then he raised his gun and I knew he was going to kill me." Lily let out a small involuntary shriek, and Saige turned, grabbing her in his arms. "He didn't, Blue, I'm here. He just brought the gun butt down on my head and knocked me out."

Lily breathed hard against his chest, then extracted herself and sat stiffly on the bale. "I don't mean to...overreact this way. I know you're here, alive." She raised her eyes to him. "I just hate to think of you—" Her voice broke.

Saige stroked her hair, nodding with understanding. "I'll try to be less graphic." He began to pace. "I came to in a room with one boarded-up window, a locked door and a straw mat on the floor." He gestured at the small space beneath the tin roof. " 'Bout this big. Except for the engines they brought me to repair, that's all I saw for seven years."

Lily nearly gagged. The idea of Saige, the most vibrant man she ever knew, locked for seven years in a windowless cell made her sick.

Behind her, Saige put his hands comfortingly on her shoulders. "It beat getting killed."

"Did they... ?" Lily reached up to cover his hand with hers. "Did they hurt you? Torture you?"

His fingers tensed, but he leaned down and pressed a gentle kiss to the top of her head. "The worst torture was being separated from you."

"You know what I mean, Saige," Lily insisted. "Did they hurt you? Did they give you enough to eat?"

"Enough to stay alive." He stepped over the bale where she sat and straddled the end of it. "You just said you don't want to hear seven years of gory details. I relived enough of that this morning with the DEA."

Lily looked at the lines etching his face that she'd grown accustomed to since his return, noticing how much more pronounced they became when he talked about this. "Go on."

"One day, about a year ago, I heard gunfire. That night a new guard came to tell me Paco was dead." Saige's voice cracked as he said the words. "I didn't know much about that place, but what

I knew I learned from Paco. I always thought his support kept me alive. Not having him around made the last year the hardest."

"Did they treat you worse?" Lily asked, unable to keep the horror from her voice.

"Periodically some organization searched the *latifundia*. I never knew who, but I imagined all kinds of entities—the Red Cross or Amnesty International or the Maraguayan government or the DEA. Maybe a rival drug lord. I never knew, and even Paco wouldn't tell me. But that last year, the visits became more frequent. I realized my captors faced some risk, or at least embarrassment, admitting they had me. And Paco was gone." Deep rage suddenly darkened Saige's expression. "That's when they really considered killing me. One of them in particular took sadistic pleasure in warning me almost every morning that that day would be my last."

Lily's mouth opened to gasp or sob or swear, but no sound came out. She could not fathom the terror Saige must have lived through.

He cupped her cheek. "Sorry. I meant to spare you that sort of detail."

She clutched his hand. "Saige, I can't comprehend. I can't..."

"Of course you can't," Saige agreed tenderly. "Besides, he was lying. I expect to spend my last day with you."

The compassion in his expression made her heart ache.

Saige continued. "Finally, one morning, Paco showed up in my room. Before I could get any answers out of him, he filled me full of drugs and... I came to at the American Embassy in Bogota."

Lily's jaw sagged. "What happened?"

"Someone must have been getting too close, so close Paco knew I hadn't a chance." He shrugged, but there was nothing nonchalant in the movement. "I'll never know the details. I'll never know exactly who they were. All I learned from Paco was that drugs came out and guns went in through the *latifundia*. The only name I ever learned was his." Saige's fists clenched so tight she thought his knuckles might crack. "I don't really even know exactly why he saved my life... or what it cost him. And now..."

Lily felt her throat tighten. "I wish I could thank him."

Saige nodded. "You can." He sat down on the other bale. "When I first returned, the drug people in Washington thought they figured out from some of the stuff I said where that *latifundia* was located. They'd been after the guy who controlled it for years. They decided to raid the place."

"Is that why you didn't tell me before?"

"Yeah." Saige looked grimly determined. "If there was even a microscopic chance it'd put you in any kind of danger, I couldn't do it." His grip on her fingers tightened. "Or Paco. They promised to try to inform him before the raid, but not if it'd risk the operation." Thunder clapped in the distance, and his gaze left hers to stare at the sky, which had grown a threatening dark gray. "He's got...had a wife and seven kids."

Suddenly Lily understood what Saige had hinted at when he mentioned finances. "How much are you going to give her, Saige?"

Saige's eyes caught hers, his expression melting to one of relief and pleasure. For the first time today, a genuine smile lit his face, easing the lines of hurt. "Not me, Blue, us. The money's part yours, which you'd know—" he shook a finger at her in mock sternness, easing some of the tension that had grown so intense "—if you'd read the property settlement."

Lily flashed him a quick grin. "You can give me a long lecture about it later."

"When Dad sold our cows, he put the money in a CD. It's been sitting in the bank, compounding and renewing itself ever since. It's quite a bit—and half yours."

"It's not, Saige. I told you, you can—"

"I'd like to give her fifty thousand dollars. In Maraguaya, that's a great deal."

"You think it's peanuts here?"

"It might even be enough for her to get out, get a better life for her and her kids. Or—"

"Do it, Saige. You're worried about my half?" Her voice rose incredulously. "Every breath you take you ... we owe to Paco. Give his wife every penny you've got, if you want."

Lily came to her feet just as Saige did. Their bodies collided as another huge clap of thunder echoed down the hillside. Lily winced and ducked farther under the tin roof. She'd been so engrossed by Saige's story, she hadn't heard the storm moving closer. The next peal exploded directly overhead, shaking the structure. Torrents of rain began to hammer against the tin.

"We've got to get out of here, Blue." Saige had to yell for her to hear him over the rain pounding on the roof and the roar of thunder all around them. "This metal roof will act like a lightning rod, and we're the ground."

When Lily didn't move immediately, Saige grabbed her arm and pulled her out into the downpour.

CHAPTER TWELVE

"OVER there," Saige hollered, pointing halfway up the hillside at an old hunter's cabin, obviously long since abandoned.

Sheets of lightning lit up the sky while thunder continued to crash. Saige tugged Lily close to his body, trying to cover her as they ran. Her gauzy skirt became rapidly soaked and droopy, tangling in her legs and tripping her repeatedly. She'd never have remained on her feet without Saige's support.

Suddenly something solid smacked her cheek. Hard white balls of ice bounced all around them and against the cows backs, making them bellow furiously. The drumbeat of hail hitting the tin roof rolled across the field toward them. Lily felt lost in chaos.

She shrieked as a hailstone the size of a golf ball hit her head. Saige pulled her tighter under his body and continued to half-carry her toward the cabin as fast as he could get her to run. Over the furor of the storm, she dimly heard him grunting in pain as hailstones struck him.

Icy water poured down her bare arms, and her skirt felt like a band of frost around her legs. Ice balls caught in her sandals and fell into her shirt between her breasts, lodging in her bra.

When at last they stumbled through the unlocked door of the cabin, Lily's teeth chattered violently. The room felt cold as winter.

"C-c-cold," she mumbled at Saige.

As ice continued to beat against the roof, Lily looked vacantly around the cabin, puzzled about exactly how they got there. If only the din of the storm would weaken, perhaps she could think clearly.

Saige, too, panted for breath. The hail had welted his cheek with two angry red abrasions, and blood oozed from a cut on his arm.

Lily reached to wipe away the blood, but her hand shook so violently she couldn't. She curled her arms tightly around her waist, unable to speak over her shivering.

Shock passed quickly over Saige's features, and he reached for her blouse. "Get out of these wet things, Blue," he said, his tone strangely urgent.

Lily nodded but couldn't seem to make her limbs move. Without hesitation, Saige pulled her blouse over her head and removed her drenched, freezing skirt. Too dazed to object, she felt him unclasp her bra and remove it, then pull off her soaking panties.

Grabbing a dirty old trapper's blanket from a cot in the corner, he shook out the excess dust and wrapped her in it tightly. Life began to come back to her fingers and toes as Saige rubbed her roughly through the blanket over every inch of her skin, front and back and up and down her arms and legs. Her teeth stopped chattering, but he didn't stop his hands. Sitting on the floor, he pulled her down onto his lap and continued his fierce massage.

Cuddling into the curve of his body, Lily felt her insides warming at last. Only then did she understand that Saige had feared she might have hypothermia.

At the moment, however, cold and fear had nothing to do with the way his hands felt on her. The warmth he generated on the outside of her body turned quickly to heat inside. Melting heat. Squirming in the tightly wrapped blanket, she managed to free her hands and press them against Saige's chest. When she felt his wet shirt, she pulled apart the buttons and pushed her hands inside against his warm skin.

Warm skin. Despite his soaking shirt and the hail, Saige's skin felt warm and his heart pounded fast beneath her fingers. Sensation and longing swamped Lily's thoughts. Frantically she sought his kiss.

As their mouths joined, his tongue delved deeply between her lips into the recesses of her mouth. Lily pushed the shirt off his shoulders, baring his chest. When she pulled her lips from his, Saige groaned with frustration. She gazed at his naked torso, trying to calm her rapid breathing, but her need for air only increased as she stared.

Remembering caresses he loved, Lily pressed her lips to the hair-covered muscles of his chest, letting her teeth graze his flat, hard nipples, nibbling lightly. The feel of his curly, intensely male hair tickling and teasing her face sent passion shuddering through every cell of her body. Her center opened to him, aching and hot and welcoming.

This was Saige! Her husband. She could not deny him, could not deny herself, another time. She had never stopped loving him, never could. Her soul had bonded with his long ago; for her, he was the essence of love. She longed to feel his life within her. Now.

"Please, Saige," she begged, her voice a trembling moan. "Love me, please, love me."

She tugged at the waistband of his jeans, desperate to remove them from his body. She wanted nothing between them but love. As Saige stood and discarded his clothes, Lily gasped with the shock of recognition. Saige was beautiful. How could she have forgotten?

He came toward her, opening the blanket and laying her on it. His hands caressed her from her hips to her breasts. Her nipples hardened into his teasing fingers, and her body arched with the need he created.

At last, Saige lowered himself over her. But as she groaned and lifted her hips toward him, he hesitated.

Lily opened her eyes to see his face above her. Tenderly he pushed the hair off her brow. He kissed her lips, drawing her tongue into his mouth.

Then he looked into her eyes. "Do you believe me now, Blue? Do you trust me?"

Lily blinked. "I don't understand." She tried to pull his weight on top of her.

"Blue," Saige groaned, resisting. "I love you, more than anything in this life. I've never wanted anything more than I want you now. But I can't just..." He closed his eyes, his face a mask of agonized frustration. "Do you want me now because you believe me? Are you ready to be my wife?"

Passion clouded Lily's mind, making rational thought impossible. She couldn't understand why Saige was asking such a question. But when the import of it came home to her, she could not make herself answer yes. What he had told her this afternoon only confirmed her certainty that adventure was the first priority in his life.

"No," she whispered. "You'll leave again, I know it." She buried her face in Saige's chest. "But I don't care. Not now. Please. I want you to love me while we still have time."

Saige swore viciously and rolled to her side. When she began to cry, he pulled her tightly into the crook of his arm.

"Don't cry, Blue," he said soothingly, stroking her still damp hair. "There'll be other times . . . if it's what you really want."

"Don't you want me?" she said at last.

"Want you! My God, how can you doubt it?" Trembling, he lifted her chin till he could see her eyes. "Don't you understand, love? I ripped your emotions to hell and back this afternoon. A few minutes ago you were almost in shock. I can't take advantage of that, no matter how much I want to." He kissed her forehead. "I don't want you to go home, take a hot bath, come to your senses and hate me. I love you too much. Blue, I can barely live with your friendship. I couldn't live if you hated me."

"I'd never hate you."

"You should if I make love to you now, when you're still not sure."

Saige stood and tucked the blanket tightly around her. Still turgid with desire, he walked toward the window and stood to one side of it gazing out the dirt-covered glass at the rain. He was completely comfortable in his nudity.

With a jolt, Lily realized she was, too, with his nudity and her own. As she watched his passion slowly fade, she knew with an unshakable intensity that she could never share the staggering intimacy of this act with any other man. She would never love another man this way. And without love this strong, the act would be an abomination.

No wonder she had put Randall off for six years. Her insides twisted with revulsion at the thought of sharing herself with Randall.

Yet more horrifying still was her knowledge that she had not lied to Saige. Though nearly overcome by passion, she'd told the stark truth: she did not trust him. She wanted to, God knows she wanted to. Yet something deep, some core of anguish built up and hardened for seven years, would not let her risk her very soul again.

But if she took Saige to her bed, she would have no choice. Her heart would not let her love him this way unless she committed herself to him wholly. Saige was right. Shock and passion had nearly overtaken her. But he had saved her deeper hurt. She loved him more for it. But she was glad he'd stopped.

Leaning her face on her bent knees, she felt herself sinking into a depression too deep for tears. She loved Saige, only Saige, always Saige. Yet she could not have him.

He crossed the room. His bare feet made soft padding sounds on the ancient floor. He knelt beside her, lifting her face.

"I'll light a fire in that old stove," he said, "and if it doesn't burn the cabin down, we'll dry our clothes."

She nodded, trying to smile.

Saige kissed the corners of her mouth. "Get those lips up," he commanded.

She tried harder, and a sort of smile did curve her mouth.

"Atta girl." He didn't sound like he wanted to smile much himself. "It's going to be okay, Blue." He cupped her cheek in his callused palm. "You'll see."

She nodded, not believing him.

He rose and turned to the stove. Within minutes, the sound of dry wood crackling began to fill the cabin and warm the small space. Saige dragged a beat-up old wooden chair and a small bench over near the stove and draped their clothes over them.

Still naked, he sent his gaze around the cabin for another covering. Finding none, he returned to Lily and joined her under the blanket.

"This is probably a terrible idea," he muttered. "But it's kind of chilly in here." He gave her a grin. "Or hadn't you noticed?"

Lily swallowed. "Not in a while."

Saige looked as tense as his knotted muscles felt next to her. He tucked the blanket between them, so that her bare skin did not touch him anywhere.

"Read any good books lately?" he asked.

The blandness of his tone amazed Lily. How could he keep himself aloof from the cyclone of emotions whooping through her? Perhaps he had learned the skill during his imprisonment.

"Saige?" she asked. "Will you answer a question?"

He forced a chuckle. "Off the record, love?"

"Don't joke."

He must have heard the intensity in her voice. "Ask away."

"What scares you about that metallic noise?"

Leaning forward stiffly, his arm across a raised knee, Saige shook his head. "No, Blue. I've answered that before." The band of muscle between his shoulder blades stretched taut as a trip wire.

"You mean you've refused to answer before." She put a hand on the tight sinews, and Saige jumped as if she'd branded him, shaking her off.

"Same thing," he growled. "That's all you'll ever hear about it."

Determinedly, Lily returned her hand to his back. He did not relax an iota. With both hands, she began to massage his shoulders and neck.

"Want to bet?" she asked. "Did you forget how stubborn I can be?"

He grunted, but no longer tried to remove her kneading hands.

Her thumbs pressed small hard circles up his neck toward his scalp. "How many hundred times do you think you can refuse me before you'll give up?"

"Before *you'll* give up," he said, his voice softening under her ministrations. "Believe me, Blue, you don't want to hear the answer. On this one, you have no choice—you *have* to trust me."

Lily believed him completely. She could not doubt that Saige's answer would horrify her to the marrow of her bones. Yet somehow she needed to know.

"I think," she said hesitantly, not quite sure how to explain to Saige or to herself, "I need to understand what you lived through. Maybe then I'll be able to believe you when you say you want to stay in Deep Water, no matter how boring."

Saige turned to her, and Lily's eyes widened in shock. He seemed to have aged ten years. "I promised myself, Blue, that I would never burden you with this." His voice sounded harsh, rough in a way she'd never heard. "You're asking to hear the worst of the whole seven years. Believe me, you'd rather not know."

Saige's anguished voice, his haunted eyes, tormented Lily. Since his return, she had thought only of how much he had hurt *her*, not what *he* must have lived through. She could no longer let him go on suffering alone.

"Tell me," she whispered, afraid of what he would reveal but determined to share it with him. "Tell me."

Indecision twisted Saige's expression, followed by guilt, then aching need. Finally he erased all emotion from his face, and his tone turned flat. "The room I lived in had a mat on the floor next to a stone wall." Saige spoke quickly as if he wanted to finish fast and banish the memory.

"Part of the wall came away, leaving a long, narrow hole."

His eyes met hers, but the glazed look in them told her he did not see her. He looked only inward, seeing again the horror he'd lived with for seven years. "When outsiders came to the *latifundia*, my guards let me know by banging on pipes. When I heard the sound, I had to hide in that hole. I never knew for how long." An expression of raging hate flashed across his face before he could control it. "It was so small, I couldn't move any part of my body. It must have been near where they threw out the kitchen garbage."

"It smelled bad?"

"The stench nearly overcame me at first, every time. But that was nothing. It drew insects, snakes, rats. My entrance disturbed them. They crawled over me, and I couldn't brush them off or move to shake them off. A few times, scorpions stung me and I was sick for days." Saige's face turned white at the memory, then ruddy with rage. "The sting burns like fire, but I couldn't make a sound. A snake bit me once, or a rat, I'm not sure. I thought I'd die from the fever that time. Hoped I would, actually, so they could never jam me in there again."

Lily put a shaking hand on his cheek. She couldn't think of a single thing to say to ease his memories.

"Once early on," he continued, his voice stronger now, "I couldn't do it. They'd forced me in there a few times, so I knew what I'd find. I had tools, because I was working on an engine. I took a wrench to the boards over the window."

"Oh, Saige!" Lily cried. "You tried to escape from drug lords who'd killed a man right before your eyes?"

"I didn't really think I could escape," he said. "I just thought I had to see some sunshine once before I got back in that hole." He touched the gray hair near his temple, hatred blazing from his eyes. "After they tried to crack my skull open, they left me in the hole for days. I figured they'd leave me there till I died. I nearly went insane."

Pressing a fist to her mouth, Lily tried to swallow, but nausea rose in her throat, fighting to emerge.

Saige pulled her against him, stiff and shaking. "I knew I shouldn't have told you," he murmured, stroking gently down her back.

"Don't!" Lily cried. "Don't you dare comfort me." She pushed his hands off her so she could wrap *him* in *her* arms. "I've given you nothing since you came home. All I've done is bitch and whine, while you—you... What you lived through... How could I be so selfish?"

"Selfish?" Saige exploded, pulling himself upright. "Don't say that." He shook her. "You've given me more than I had any right to expect."

"What are you talking about?" Lily said, her throat tight from fighting tears. "I gave you noth—"

"You waited for me, Blue." Saige's emotion-filled voice echoed in the tiny cabin. "You can pretend all you want about getting engaged and going on with your life. But you waited for me. Sooner or later—" he lifted his shoulders in a tense, jerky shrug "—you'll know it. You couldn't have given me more."

The tumult of emotions Lily fought to control overcame her. Reaching for Saige, she enfolded him again in her embrace. Tears began to stream from her eyes. She leaned her cheek on the top of his head, soaking his damp hair with salty drops. Slowly the tension drained out of him.

Finally he straightened slightly so he could see her face. "Hey, Blue," he said, sounding slightly stunned.

"What?" She sniffed, trying to dry her tears with the stiff old blanket.

"Thanks." Saige wiped her cheeks with his knuckle. "I never thought I'd tell anyone that." He pulled in a long breath and let it out slowly. "I guess I needed to. It feels different now, as if maybe I can let it go."

Lily pulled him close again. "I hope so. I'd love to believe I helped."

"More than you know."

She tightened her arms around him.

"Blue?"

"Mm?"

"Did you change your mind about making love?" He slid his arms around her waist. "Because if you didn't, we'd better get dressed."

Lily snuggled tighter into Saige's warmth, not wanting to answer, not even wanting to *think* about the answer. How could she know if she'd changed her mind? Her mind wouldn't release her from her emotions long enough to let her form rational thoughts. Love for her husband and a deep longing to heal his wounds filled her. But so did fear for herself, for taking that final step again and giving her whole heart to him.

Of *course* his story had affected her profoundly. She couldn't hear it and keep fully intact the barricade of reserve she'd built around her heart. But did that mean she really believed at last that a man who'd lived through such torture would never again want to leave the security of his home? Could she really believe Saige had grown up at last? A man who could risk his life just to look at sunlight?

Could she? Was she ready at least to try? Lily pressed her face against the comfort of Saige's throat. She tried to lace her fingers together behind his head, but he took her shoulders and held her away from him. Clearly he would not let passion make this decision for her.

"I want all of you, Blue." There was nothing weak or indecisive in the set of his jaw, the tenor of his voice. "Not just your body."

Saige's arm's-length grip, the chilly room cooling her ardor, brought Lily to the present with an unpleasant jolt. Somehow her first thought was for Randall, the man she remained engaged to. Though Lily knew she and Randall had to talk about ending their engagement, they had not done so yet.

She frowned. He might not be the right man for her, but he had never hurt her and he had helped her a great deal. Surely she owed him the faithfulness she'd promised until she decided otherwise.

Saige gave a chuckle of self-deprecation. "All that indecision, love, is terribly complimentary." He leaned forward and gave her a brotherly peck on the tip of her nose before pulling her to her feet. "I'll get our clothes."

CHAPTER THIRTEEN

BY THE time Lily returned to the pickup, her damp clothes clung to her, chilling her all over again. Rain drizzled from an iron gray sky, blowing in gusts against her face and body. Though Saige kept his arm around her waist holding her close, she couldn't stop shivering.

But her overloaded brain had long since ceased to notice anything as mundane as shivering. A welcome numbness had also eclipsed hurt, guilt, passion, joy and even love. She fumbled with the door handle, thinking only of the heater inside and the pleasures of hot water awaiting her at home.

Saige opened the door for her, then climbed in the driver's side. "Shall I take you home?"

"T-to my c-car," she said. "I'll be fine."

"Fine, love?" A half grin cocked his lips. "You look like a tractor ran over you. I'm not sure you should be alone just now." He tenderly touched the swollen skin below her eyes. "I keep making you cry, Blue, and I don't like to think of you crying by yourself."

Lily pulled in a long breath. "I d-don't have any tears left, Saige. I think this is what they mean b-by burnout. I don't plan to feel a thing for days." She pushed soggy hair off her brow. "I have to d-do some thinking, alone. Pen offered me a leave of absence. I'm going to take it."

"Where will you go?" Saige asked, his forehead creasing with worry as he turned onto the highway. "I'd like to make sure you get there safely."

"I'm fine," Lily repeated, feeling life return to her toes as the truck's heater warmed them. "And you are the last person...well, maybe the next-to-last person I'd tell where I'm going."

She said nothing more till Saige stopped the pickup outside the newspaper office where she'd parked her car. She jumped out, slipped quickly behind the wheel of her car and reached to pull her door shut.

Saige held it open. "Blue—"

"I'll see you in a few days, Saige, and..."

He let her pull the door from his fingers. "And...?"

"I don't know," Lily cried. "I don't know." She slammed the door and drove away.

Without making a conscious decision, Lily drove to Dana's house, her childhood home, instead of her apartment.

"Baby!" Dana pulled her inside. "What happened to you?"

Lily fell into the haven of his arms. "What didn't?" she said. "Can I hole up here a few days, Dad? In secret?"

"Of course," Dana said. "But who are you hiding from? Saige or Randall?"

"I'm not sure," Lily admitted, making a beeline for the bathroom.

"If you're hiding from yourself, Lil—" Dana's tone, kind and understanding though it was, reminded Lily of other times he'd kept her from self-deception "—it won't work." He followed her, handing her a clean towel from the linen closet. "We'll talk when you're warm and dry."

An hour later, wrapped in Dana's wool plaid bathrobe, sipping a cup of his hot fruit soup, Lily had an answer for him. "I'm hiding from everyone *but* me, Dad. I have to make this decision myself." She reached for his hand. "With no input from anyone else, even you."

Dana nodded. "You should have done this a month ago, baby. I won't say a word, except what do you want for dinner?"

For the first time in weeks, Lily felt her muscles really relax. The storm of conflicting emotions that had held her heart in a vise since she'd seen Saige at the parade began to let go. Suddenly she was so sleepy, she couldn't keep her eyes open. With a feeling of utter security, she rose and propelled her tired body toward her childhood bed.

* * *

The following Saturday, Lily returned to her apartment to dress for the end-of-summer banquet at the golf course. Because she'd already promised Pen, who wanted two full pages of pictures, she hadn't even tried to get out of covering it, but she did not look forward to the event.

Last year at this party, she and Randall had announced their engagement. Tonight she feared they would end it. She had called Randall earlier, trying to break their formal date, hoping he'd agree just to meet her at the clubhouse. But he refused.

"My car's in the shop," he said. "I'm spending the weekend at Mother's while Dad's visiting. I need you to pick me up at their place. We'll have a drink with Mother and Dad before we go."

Lily's heart sank.

By yesterday afternoon, she'd known her time of hiding had to end soon. She had reached all the conclusions she could alone. Only two were worth noting.

One, she would not marry Randall simply out of gratitude. Troubling though it was to admit, she suspected that was all she'd ever felt for him. Perhaps it would have been enough if Saige hadn't returned and reminded her with such intensity how much more love could mean. She could no longer pretend that she and Randall had, or ever could have, the kind of relationship she used to share with Saige.

Two, she didn't trust Saige yet, and couldn't in so short a time. But she wished to trust him. Dear heaven, she ached for it till she thought her heart would burst.

Lily didn't know what Randall had told his parents about her absence the last few days. She didn't care. But she did not look forward to having their reunion at Kokie's house and trying to mix serious talk with a lot of social chitchat.

Resigning herself to her fate, Lily donned the shimmering midnight blue evening dress she'd purchased for the dance. Until she slipped it over her head and let its slithery fabric droop across her bosom, she hadn't realized how much weight she'd lost this summer worrying about Saige. The neckline sagged ridiculously between her breasts and gaped open.

Lily stared at the mirror, wondering whether to laugh or cry. Laughter won easily. She'd shed far too many tears this summer over something that mattered to worry about a misfitting dress.

As she gazed dejectedly into her closet, Lily's desire to laugh faded. Hers was a typical Montana closet, three-quarters winter clothes with only a scattering of lightweight garb. She wore evening clothes once a year at most, and had a meager selection to choose from.

It took her less than ten minutes to try on everything even remotely suitable. To her dismay, Lily found only one wearable dress, a dark red silk gown that draped in togalike folds from one shoulder, leaving the other bare to just above her breast. Turning to examine herself in the mirror, she knew Randall would not approve of all that exposed skin and even less the slit up her skirt from ankle to mid-thigh.

Lily shrugged philosophically. It could be worse, she thought, securing her long blond hair to the sides of her head with jeweled combs. At least Randall couldn't tell by looking that Saige had given her the dress for Christmas the year they lived in New York.

Remembering that New Year's Eve made Lily's eyes sting, and she blinked rapidly, nearly destroying her mascara. As they'd descended to the subway station in evening clothes, Saige had responded to the stares they'd received by playing the part of the perfect British butler. When he called her "medem" and bowed her into the subway car, Lily had convulsed with laughter. She blinked again, wondering if Saige would remember the dress, and the evening, with such clarity.

Fluttering her lashes against a tissue to dry them, Lily made herself calm down. What did it matter what Saige *or* Randall thought? She had nothing else to wear. And she had to admit, as she examined herself once more in the mirror, it *was* the most beautiful dress she'd ever owned.

When she shut off her car's motor in Kokie's circular driveway, Lily glanced at the huge diamond ring on her finger, knowing what she had to do. Her major hurdle was getting through the next hour of stilted conversation. She mounted the steps and entered the foyer without bothering to knock.

As she approached the archway to the living room, she heard Kokie's voice. Lily hesitated, steeling herself.

"...perfectly disgraceful the way she looks at him," Kokie was saying. "The talk has grown more embarrassing every week since the man's unfortunate return from the dead."

Lily choked with horror at hearing Saige's precious human life described as "unfortunate." Yet Randall began speaking as if his mother had said nothing untoward.

"Surely, Mother—" his voice floated out to Lily sounding only vaguely uncomfortable with the subject "—you don't expect me to let small-town gossip influence my choice of a wife."

"Of course not," Kokie said. "Not if you truly love her."

"You know how I feel."

"Then you must see that the man's presence in Deep Water will exert a constant strain on your marriage." The sounds of crystal clinking against crystal, liquid splashing into a glass, told Lily Kokie had refilled her cocktail with Scotch from the decanter.

"I think it extremely unlikely he'll remain in Deep Water," Randall said. "Our marriage, on top of the tedium of ranching, will be just the impetus he needs to begin wandering again."

"Your marriage will have the reverse effect, I'm afraid." Lily wondered how Kokie could sound so confident about a man she'd seen for only a few tense moments at the rodeo. "I, um, he... Believe me, Saige Alexander has no intention of leaving." Kokie's glass clinked onto a Limoges coaster. "So if you wish to have a decent marriage, you'll have to."

"Have to?"

"Leave, dear. I'm sure your old law partners would welcome you back."

Randall gave a self-deprecatory chuckle. "Indeed they would, since it would assure the firm they'd continue to have Dad's business. But Lillabeth—"

"Lily can work with me at the charitable trust," Kokie interrupted. "We can always use women with her organization skills to plan benefits."

Lily felt faint. Join Kokie's social whirl in California? She couldn't imagine anything worse—even if she wanted to leave Deep Water, which she most certainly didn't. But Randall knew that, and would tell Kokie so now.

"I suppose you're right, Mother," Randall said. "Deep Water's charm has paled for me the last year. I'm sure Lillabeth will understand I need to make the move for my career." He made a noise Lily supposed he meant to be a laugh.

"After we're married, of course she'll have to follow her husband's wishes."

If Kokie said something else, Lily didn't hear it. The last vestiges of the love she felt for Randall seemed to wither and die at his words. She no longer felt a need to break it to him gently. If Randall truly loved her even a little, he could not have said those things. A sensation of unreality swept over her—as if the whole six years of their relationship had been based on something false.

On legs that felt like wood, Lily entered the living room. "Randall," she began. "I—we..."

"My dear." Randall leaped to his feet, red suffusing his neck above the stiff white collar of his boiled shirt. "How long..."

"Long enough." Lily pulled the diamond ring off her finger and put it on the cocktail tray beside Kokie's decanter. "There's your ring. Do I need to explain why I'm returning it?"

Randall gaped at it. "You've never worn it before," he said obtusely.

"It never fit," Lily said. "I see that now. It fits here. I don't."

She stared at the platinum and diamond ring winking up at her from the sterling silver tray next to the lead crystal decanter with its sterling silver label. They all fit together—beautiful and rich and...cold. Love and warmth had no place in this setting.

"Perhaps I'll see you at the golf course." She stepped back, out of range of Randall's outstretched hands. "But you'll forgive me if I don't save you a dance."

"Lillabeth, please," he said. "Let me drive you to the banquet so we can talk. You owe me that, at least."

"I owe you one thing," Lily replied. "Thanks for getting me off the ranch and convincing Pen to hire me." Randall's stricken look caused her only a moment's remorse. "Randall, sleep on this and you'll know I'm right. Even hearing you wanted to take me from my home against my will caused me more shock than real dismay. Believe it or not, this has nothing to do with Saige."

With that Lily spun on her heel and left a sputtering Randall with his adoring mother. Why had she never realized before how much alike they were?

She had just opened her car door when Randall ran onto the porch after her. "Lillabeth," he called, "you don't really mean this, do you? It can't just be over between us. What about the invitations?"

Lily gaped at him. Was it his lawyer's training that made him want everything in triplicate?

"Randall," she said, speaking very clearly. "We are through, our engagement is terminated." She paused with her foot on the frame of the car, though the movement exposed most of her nylon-covered leg. "Have one of your mother's organization women retract the invitations."

With a surge of relief so strong it shocked her, Lily sped down Kokie's drive faster than she'd ever gone in Randall's Lamborghini.

Lily wormed her way through the crushing crowd, accepting compliments on her dress with a pleasure she hadn't expected to feel tonight. With relief she stepped out through the wide glass door onto the porch. Camera in hand, she leaned against the railing and looked at the lines of people around the bar and what looked like two-thirds of Deep Water's population milling together on the dance floor.

A stir at the front door caught her attention. By some fluke of coincidence, Saige was entering at the same moment as Randall and his parents. The band continued to play, but conversation throughout the small clubhouse fell silent while Randall, ever polite, made introductions.

Kokie, her brows raised nearly to her hairline, stared at Saige's outstretched hand, then lifted her chin disdainfully and turned away. Slipping one hand to her husband's elbow and the other to her son's, she moved regally toward the bar.

To a chorus of chuckles, Saige examined his hand carefully, turning one side up, then the other, as if to make sure he hadn't missed something. Finally he shrugged and grinned at Kokie's retreating back. There was no malice in the smile, but even from the porch, Lily noted a hint of triumph.

Then Saige turned, stepping out of the shadow of the entrance. Lily's breathing quickened as his eyes sought her in the crowd. Saige's six weeks at home had transformed him from that pale, cadaverous man she'd seen at the parade. His sunstreaked hair fell across his tanned brow and glinted golden against the black collar of his dinner jacket. His pleated shirt fit perfectly across his deep muscular chest, narrowing over his flat belly covered by the dark red cummerbund.

At last he saw Lily, standing at the railing. His gaze swept once up and down the red silk dress, and a smile of recognition slowly spread across his tanned features.

In formal clothes, he looked stunningly handsome. Every female eye in the clubhouse followed him as he moved through the crush of old friends, never taking his gaze from Lily. She felt like Cinderella pursued by the prince and stood motionless, afraid to break the spell.

At last he neared her. "Dance?"

She couldn't speak.

Removing the camera from her fingers, Saige placed it on the railing then pulled her into his arms and onto the dance floor, where the crowd of other dancers pushed them close together. Lily slipped naturally into his embrace, her body molding to his as if it belonged there.

I do belong here, she thought, leaning her head on his shoulder. *In these arms, with this man, I belong here... forever.*

A hundred memories of dances with Saige assailed her. But when he curled their hands together on his chest and pressed his other hand low on her spine, the memories fled, overcome by the power of the moment.

This was no teenage boy or carefree graduate student who held her to him. Saige was all man now, his body filled out and hardened by ranch work, his heart gentled by suffering, more full of love than ever before. He was every inch the man she knew, yet different. Harder yet softer, stronger yet more vulnerable.

And she loved him! So much she could hardly draw a proper breath.

His ear was inches from her mouth. Her heart urged her to pour out her love for him as she had in high school. She opened her lips to do so. But the words lodged in her throat, felled by the rational thought that said "forever" had never meant the same thing to Saige as it did to her.

Saige's heat flowed into her as he moved their bodies slowly together in time with the music. "Why'd you wear this dress, Blue?"

"I..." Lily shrugged, striving for a casualness she didn't feel. "It fit."

"Fit?" Saige slid his hands down her spine. "You've lost weight, haven't you? Ten..." He cupped her bottom briefly in his palms. He grinned, but his voice came out serious. "About twelve pounds?"

"Mm," she said, letting her hands roam over his broad back. "And you've gained—" she returned the favor of a quick massage of his buttocks "—at least twenty-two."

"Bingo," Saige murmured. Beneath his stiff shirt, his heart beat a staccato rhythm she could feel against her breasts. "You didn't need to lose any weight, Blue. I liked you kind of—" his hands stroked her from waist to hips "—fleshy."

"Fleshy!" Lily raised her head from his shoulder and slapped his hands. "Keep your hands to yourself, you lecher."

Laughing, Saige ignored her, continuing his gentle exploration of her body. "I like to think of you getting bigger and bigger, here," he whispered, moving one hand between them to caress her belly over her womb, "with our child."

A pulsing low inside her, just below Saige's questing hands, made Lily ache from seven years of unquenched want. With a soft moan, she twisted hard against his unyielding, undeniably masculine body.

His lips covered her ear, breathing warmly. "You never know, though," he whispered. "The kid may turn out a complete monster. No guarantees in life, Blue." His tongue teased the whorls inside her ear.

"Saige," Lily begged, breathless from his ministrations, clinging to his shoulders to remain upright. "Please stop, we're on the dance floor."

Saige nodded. "Surrounded by too many people for anyone to notice a thing." But he returned his hand to the small of her back. "Blue?" he asked, when she rested her head on him again.

With her heart pounding loud in her ears, Lily couldn't be sure, but she thought he sounded hesitant, which seemed odd. Her knees trembled almost as if he'd made love to her on the dance floor. He'd talked of childbearing and the size of her body as if they were alone...in bed. What would make him bashful now?

"What, Saige?"

"Did you come alone tonight?" His arm at the back of her waist tensed. "Not with Carver?"

"Yes. No." She raised her head to meet his eyes. "I mean, yes, I didn't come with Randall. I drove out to Kokie's to get him, because his car's in the shop, and then he and Kokie..."

Lily stopped because she was babbling. Saige didn't care about Kokie, and the expectant look in his eyes faded at the mere mention of her name. Lily glanced at the other dancers around them, wishing they could go someplace more private. But even the porch was crowded now.

Oh, no! Her gaze flicked to the porch. Pen stood just outside the door, snapping pictures of dancers with *her* camera. After everything else he'd put up with from her this summer, now he was even doing her job for her. It was too much.

Lily tried to disentangle herself from Saige's grasp, which felt suddenly as secure as an octopus's. "Saige," she said, "let me go. I've got work to do." She gestured toward the decorated buffet and the nearly empty dining room with the tables still attractively set. "Before the destruction begins."

"Pen's making you work tonight?" Saige grumbled.

"I offered," she explained, moving toward the porch and her camera. "This Thursday's is *the* issue of the year for most of the summer people."

"Hi, Pen," Saige said, as Lily drew them near. He slanted her a mischievous grin. "I hope you got a shot of my hand on her tush."

"Saige!" Lily said, blushing in front of Pen. Grabbing her camera, she left the men alone.

Lily sagged against the bar, leaning her elbows on the padded rim. She would never agree to cover this dinner dance again. Since she had retrieved her camera from Pen, she had not sat down for a second. She'd eaten off a plate at the bar, a bite here, a bite there, till the food was unpalatably cold.

She'd talked to a hundred people, politely avoiding an explanation of why she hadn't come to the dance with Randall. As the evening wore on, the explanation became more and more superfluous, for Randall danced with every available woman at the party. He seemed indefatigable in making sure that his steps took him and his partner within range of Lily's lens. She couldn't count the number of photographs he'd ruined tonight.

She sipped her fourth Shirley Temple, remembering last year's dance. Randall had insisted that she refuse to work that night. She had drunk champagne instead of lemonade. Randall had announced their engagement, and she'd danced every dance with him.

With another long pull at her drink, Lily admitted she was having more fun tonight than she had last year. She'd felt treasured then, cossetted, protected, safe. But all that protection had also confined her, constricted her...controlled her! Like telling Pen she wouldn't work—that had been Randall's idea, not hers.

She understood that her unreasonable fear of abandonment had very nearly let her make the mistake of a lifetime. Whether or not Saige actually settled down, his return had rescued her from a marriage made anywhere but in heaven. Perhaps she should have told him on the dance floor that she had returned Randall's ring.

But she wanted to say *more* than that. Wanted Saige to understand that she did love him, desperately, she just wasn't ready to trust yet. And she knew that the ensuing discussion—of just what signal she was waiting for—would not make her comfortable. Because she had no answer. And she had *not* wanted to start arguing—or crying— in the middle of a party.

Saige's voice behind her interrupted her thoughts. Looking around, Lily saw his back. He stood at the bar with Ran Carver, waiting to attract the attention of the bartender.

"...real problem down there," Saige was saying, "is the inflation rate, which can eat up your profits before you get them out of the country and back into dollars."

"That's true," Ran agreed. "But what's the solution?"

"Solution?" Saige laughed. Lily was surprised to hear his laughter sound so natural. Just as she always had, Saige must feel at ease with Randall's father.

"We have to stop thinking of lesser developed countries as storehouses for natural resources we want to appropriate," Saige said, "and an underpaid work force we can exploit."

The conversation turned to economics, and Lily quit listening to take a photo of an elderly couple who had not missed an end-of-summer banquet since the first one, thirty-eight years ago in Elly Wren's barn. As she watched the couple move onto the dance floor, Lily was filled with envy for their fifty-four-year marriage.

And yet, their marriage undoubtedly appeared more comfortable now, looking back at it, than it had felt living it. He had left her alone on the ranch for three years to fight in World War Two. Their oldest son had lost the use of his arm in a tractor accident, and a few years ago their new calving shed had burned to the ground.

Saige was right—life offered no guarantees. Pen had said that, too. Everyone seemed to know it but Lily.

Is *that* what she was waiting for from Saige—a guarantee? If so, she asked too much. Just because fate had dealt her one very cruel blow didn't mean she'd earned a place in Shangri-la for the rest of her life.

Lily should have spent the past six weeks rejoicing in Saige's return, not indulging her hurts and testing his faithfulness. Her love for him transcended everything else in her life. Being with him, sharing his life—for however long she could—was worth a risk, *any* risk.

"...like you're just the man we're looking for." Ran's voice snapped Lily's attention to her eavesdropping. "I need to slow down. The board of directors and I decided we need a younger man to troubleshoot for the corporation. We've got offices in thirty-three countries, South America, Asia, Europe. The job would require a lot of travel."

Lily's heart stuttered to a halt, then raced as if it would never catch up. She wanted to gag Ran, make the world back up, forcing his awful words back inside his mouth.

He had just offered Saige the job of his dreams, traveling the world for pay. He'd *never* have to settle down. As far as Saige knew, Lily was still engaged to Randall. He had nothing to keep him here. She would lose him again, and this time she knew she would not survive the loss.

No! her heart screamed. She would *not* lose him. She'd already decided. Saige's love was worth any risk. She wouldn't let him go—not without her. If Saige left Deep Water, she'd be at his side. In fact, she doubted she'd ever let him out of her sight again.

But Saige was shaking his head. Shaking his head? Lily gripped the edge of the bar for support. Saige was shaking his head!

"I appreciate the offer, sir," Saige said to Ran. "But I have a job here." A tinge of excitement entered his voice. "I bought a herd of black baldies today, the most beautiful herd in the state. The only thing I ever plan to export is beef, raised by me on my ranch." Saige's shoulders tensed, straining the seams of his dinner jacket. "I wanted to raise a bunch of little Alexanders, too. But I think I blew my chances for that."

Lily forgot her wish not to cry at a party. Tears of joy streamed down her face. The mascara she'd worked so hard to get right must be leaving awful streaks down her cheeks. She wanted to speak, but a huge lump closed her throat.

She took a wobbly step toward him, and Ran noticed her over Saige's shoulder. "Actually, young man, I believe your chances are better than you think."

Saige spun around and saw her. His eyes squeezed shut as a look of intense joy and relief crossed his face, then snapped open as if he was afraid she'd disappear. "Now, Blue? You believe me now?"

Taking her face between his palms, he kissed her eyes, her temples, her lips, softly, gently, with pure love, no demand. The gentleness lasted only a moment. Lily's hunger flared, and she locked her fingers together behind Saige's neck, pulling him closer. For a time, Lily didn't know how long, he indulged her need. However long he kissed her, it ended too soon and left her trembling in his arms.

"Not here," he muttered, his voice hoarse as he took his lips from hers. He gazed at her, his eyes glistening suspiciously. "Blue, God, Blue, I love you so much."

"Saige, I would have said yes anyway," she said. "If you really want to, take this job. I'll go around the world with you."

"True Blue," Saige murmured. "There is only one place on this earth you are going with me." His voice dropped huskily. "Home."

His arms tightened around her, then he hesitated. "I haven't bought any...that is, the drug store's closed by now...." He softly touched her lips with his. "Blue, will you mind very much if you get pregnant tonight?"

"Mind?" Lily cried, laughing with sheer joy. "Oh, Saige! Mind?" She pressed a row of kisses across his neck.

Saige's chuckle resounded with male satisfaction. "I guess you don't mind."

Lifting her in his arms, Saige took her home again.

HARLEQUIN PRESENTS®

So who were the Brodeys?

**Money, looks, style. The Brodey family
had everything...except love**

in

**Sally Wentworth's exciting three-part series
TIES OF PASSION**

Read Calum Brodey's story in

#1843 CALUM

Harlequin Presents—the best has just
gotten better!

Available in October wherever Harlequin books
are sold.

HARLEQUIN PRESENTS®

Love can conquer the deadliest of

The compelling seven-part series by

Charlotte Lamb

Coming next month:

#1840 DARK FEVER
the sin of Lust

Gil Marquez opened up feelings of intense desire in
Bianca that she didn't know she possessed. How could
she want him with such dark intensity, yet be certain
that she was falling in love...?

Available in October wherever
Harlequin books are sold.

SINS5

**Sabrina   It Happened One Night
Working Girl   Pretty Woman
While You Were Sleeping**

If you adore romantic comedies then have
we got the books for you!

Look for Harlequin's
LOVE & LAUGHTER™
at your favorite retail outlet. It's a brand-new
series with two books every month capturing
the lighter side of love.

You'll enjoy humorous love stories by favorite
authors and brand-new writers, including
JoAnn Ross, Lori Copeland, Jennifer Crusie,
Kasey Michaels and many more!

As an added bonus—with the purchase, at
retail, of two new Love & Laughter books you
can receive a **free** copy of our fabulous
Love and Laughter collector's edition.

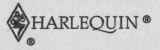

LOVE & LAUGHTER™—a natural
combination...always
romantic...always entertaining

◆HARLEQUIN ®

Look us up on-line at: http://www.romance.net

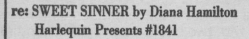